THE DREAD SOUTH

THE

DEVIL

OWNS

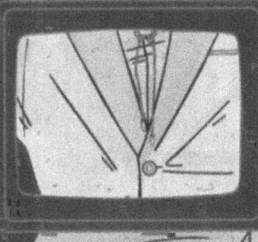

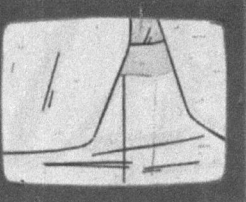

PRIMETIME

SIRIUS

THE DEVIL OWNS PRIMETIME
A Dread South Novella

SIRIUS

THE LAUGHING MAN HOUSE PUBLISHING

This book is a work of fiction. References to real people, events, establishments, organizations, or locales are intended only to provide a sense of authenticity, and are used to advance the fictional narrative. All other characters, and all incidents and dialogue, are drawn from the author's imagination and are not to be construed as real.

THE DEVIL OWNS PRIMETIME

This book is dedicated, unironically, to Pat Robertson.
You never knew me, but you hated me.
And I outlived you.

ALSO BY SIRIUS

The Draonir Saga
Uncrowned
Partitioned
Condemned
Disinherited*

The Draonir Saga: Iconoclasts
Hawthorne: A Draonir Novella
The Red Star Society

The Gentlemen Demon Series
Swallow You Whole
Sever Your Spine

The Wire Killers Novellas
Birdeater

The Dread South Series
Rising Sun Over the Devil's Nest
Blackjack + Moonshine
Gospel of the Cuckoo
Funny Little Town
Late Night Testament

*TBA

CHAPTER ONE

LIGHT OF
THE WORLD

The handsome face on the TV screen took up all 25 inches of burning phosphors. And rightfully so, in Josiah's opinion. The picture was clear as a damn bell to where he could see everything down to the beads of sweat on his upper lip, glistening on the ends of his dark, neatly trimmed mustache. No one else would notice, he was sure, on their little

13-inch screens where the little rainbow lines rippled across the picture—but he was a details man. He always had been.

He spread his legs a little wider and switched the speed of his magic wand to *'high'.* The long white cord snaked around his thigh and disappeared around the side of the couch where he had unplugged the floor lamp to make sure he could get some much-needed *quiet time.* The vibrator was loud as hell, sounding like a goddamn belt sander, and he could hardly hear himself over the buzz. Josiah grabbed the boxy TV remote with his free hand and hit the second button to turn up the volume.

Shit. He pushed the head of the wand down onto his cock. *Clit. Cock. What the fuck ever.* He loved the way his earring sparkled under the television lights. A single diamond-studded cross that pierced his right lobe making a simple but bold statement. He had a nice jawline, too. It looked especially sharp from whatever camera angle the broadcast had caught. Sideburns did him favors. So did the facial hair. He was so goddamn attractive. He angled the wand back up twisted it a little. A ray of pleasure shot through him and he clenched his teeth, holding back a moan as he turned the TV up again until it hit its highest volume bar.

"AND AS IT SAYS IN THE GOOD BOOK OF REVELATION," his voice finally filled the room, resonant over the buzzing wand with just enough Texas running his words together to appease the locals. "THAT GOD WILL PUNISH THE SINNER. HE WILL PUNISH THE LIAR. HE WILL PUNISH THE THIEF WHO COMES IN THE NIGHT. HE WILL PUNISH THE HOMOSEXUALS AND HE WILL PUNISH THE NON-BELIEVER. I SAY TO YOU, CHURCH, THAT GOD IS HERE IN THIS HOUSE TONIGHT AND HE BRINGS THE ROD OF JUDGMENT! FOR MY GOD *IS* THE OLD TESTAMENT GOD! THE GOD OF ABRAHAM—"

SHIT! Another bone-rattling quiver of pleasure shot through him and soaked through his thin cotton boxers. The head of his wand was getting shiny and slick, but it kept on like a trooper. He wished it had a higher setting. He started moving it up and down, grinding it against his cock. The version of him that was on the TV smiled and shouted towards the choir of 30 navy-robed gospel singers standing towards the back of the stage.

"PRAISE GOD! AMEN!"

3

"Amen! Fuck!" Josiah threw his head back and squeezed his thighs around his wand. He rode the head, panting as his orgasm erupted between his legs and made his hole tight and his legs shake. He moaned and finally withdrew the wand, shoving his fingers through the opening in the front of his boxers and stroking his throbbing, swollen, drenched cock until the last of the orgasm had ebbed away.

The front door opened and Josiah pushed a disgruntled sound through his teeth. He yanked the magic wand cord out of the wall and fell back into the couch cushions, spreading his arms across the back.

On the other side of the dividing wall, he caught sight of his boyfriend's head. A familiar sight of unruly dark hair tucked underneath a corduroy cap and oversized, coke-bottle lens glasses that made him look so wide-eyed all the time. Theo was a modern marvel in the sense that he was so attractive, but never on purpose. He was modest and unassuming, and it was all very endearing. But he also had a habit of spoiling Josiah's afternoons by traipsing through the house with no consideration for his private time.

"Goddamn it, Theo!" Josiah called out.

4

"I'm sorry, Rev," Theo apologized immediately, like he had walked in with one already prepared. "I didn't realize you were home."

"Would there be another Corvette parked in this driveway?" Josiah snorted.

"No, Rev, you're right. I'm sorry." Theo disappeared from sight and into the kitchen. There was a rustling of paper bags, what Josiah assumed to be groceries. "Do you mind—I'm sorry—do you mind turning the TV down? I can't hear you from in here."

"Well, that might be because I didn't say anything." Josiah turned the volume down on the TV nonetheless and stood up. He grabbed the front of his boxers and straightened them up before heading towards the kitchen, lingering in the doorway and leaning with one arm against the frame.

Theo was already busy unpacking the grocery bags, moving back and forth between the tables and the cabinet like a zipping honeybee.

"Did you park behind me?" Josiah asked. "I am preaching tonight at the church. Then I am going by the studio after."

"I did. I'll move my car." Theo said. "Will you eat dinner here before you go?" He paused in

5

his zooming to walk up to the reverend with his chin tilted upward for a kiss.

Josiah grabbed that ugly corduroy hat and whipped it off his boyfriend's head before leaning down to kiss him. "Not likely," he said. "I probably won't be home another hour. I'm going to shower then get going."

"Oh." Theo seemed a bit deflated. He lingered in front of Josiah, resting a hand against his chest and playing with the silver-plated cross that dangled from his neck. "You need to eat *something*. You get mean when you don't eat."

Josiah rolled his eyes. "I'll pick up something on the way." He tossed the hat onto the kitchen table and straightened his posture. "I assume you're not going to beg me to tag along?" He sneered.

Theo furrowed his brow and adjusted his glasses. "You know how I feel about organized religion, Rev," he said. "And I don't think there's a single soul in your congregation who, well—let's just say if I caught fire, I don't think one of them would piss on me to put it out."

"It's because you are a *homo-sex-ual*," Josiah drew the word out and prodded his boyfriend in the chest. "They can tell, you know."

"Can they?" Theo's brow shot back up incredulously. "But you've got them all fooled?"

"You think they've got my number?" Josiah flashed a smile and fingered the cross around his neck. "I don't think so. That's what I've got Pollyanna for."

Theo's mouth shriveled and he turned away. He shuffled back over to the kitchen table and pulled out a few cardboard boxes of pasta that he stuffed into the pantry. "I think they know more than you want to believe. They just care about the ratings more than some *faggot* jumping around behind their pulpit."

A growl like thunder rolled its way up Josiah's throat. For half a second, the only relief he could imagine for the tight knot inside his chest was the image of Theo's pretty face getting slammed into the side of the refrigerator.

He shook it free. He did not have time for that.

"Just move the Buick," Josiah snarled as he turned away. "And don't wait up. I'll be late. I left the TV on, so don't turn it off. I don't care if you watch tonight's broadcast, but it pumps the numbers up to leave it running."

"I know, I know," Theo said. He sounded defeated, but Josiah wasn't up to giving him any comfort. He would kiss it better when he got home—maybe, if he felt like it.

Josiah stripped off his tank top on his way to the shower and left his lover behind in the kitchen. He left his dirty clothes on the bed, which he knew Theo hated. But he could not give less of a shit.

The *Last Chance for Faith* Church was an enormous white building with too many uncovered windows and a nearly inaccessible parking lot. The church's maximum capacity sat at a modest 30,000, but whoever had been tasked with painting the white lines had probably done a few bumps of cocaine to get him going beforehand. The parking spaces were all over the place and there were only three locations for getting in and out. Josiah didn't have to worry about that, though, because his parking space was labelled. It had "REVEREND JOSIAH TUCKER" printed on a white aluminum sign and it was right by the front door.

He stepped out of his cherry-red Corvette and used a handkerchief to swing the door shut. Smudges and fingerprints were two things he hated, especially on his freshly waxed car. He needed to be able to see his face in the tinted passenger windows at all times.

Josiah reached into his white suit jacket and pulled out the brown leather cigar case he kept tucked in the silk-lining pocket. There were at least two 'No Smoking' signs posted on either side of the front doors, but those were for the rednecks who smoked cheap menthols.

Josiah clipped the end of his cigar and lit it up before walking into the building. A rush of air conditioning hit him in the face and brought with it the smell of bleach and floor cleaner. A clean church was a Godly church, and the fumes made him giddy. He released a cloud of smoke into the atmosphere and tucked the end of his cigar into the corner of his mouth as he kept going.

"Good afternoon, Reverend." Ollie, one of the church board deacons, came out to greet him. He coughed a bit at the smoke but smothered the sound with his hand.

Josiah flashed him a grin that made the cigar bob. "Good afternoon, deacon," he said. He liked to pretend that he couldn't remember all their names. It really wasn't important, and they didn't expect him to, anyway. "Fine day that the Lord has made."

"Oh, yes. A fine day." Ollie smiled back. It took a lot for a man to praise the Lord when he was sweating bullets in a three-piece suit. There was a reason he was on the church board. "If you have a moment, Reverend, I would like to talk to you about this year's Christmas program."

"Isn't it August, now?" Josiah asked. He huffed another cloud of smoke, funneling it through his nostrils.

"Well, yes." Ollie adjusted the thick-rimmed glasses that sat on the bridge of his sloped nose. "But it's never too early in the year to plan. The board narrowed down all the charity candidates to its top three and we would like you to have the final word on who we sponsor. Then of course there is the children's..."

"I get it." Josiah waved his hand. "You can leave all that with Pollyanna and I'll take a look tonight. I'm headed up to the studio right after the sermon for the primetime hour broadcast, so I'll take a gander after that."

"Bless you." Ollie grinned. "What is the subject matter tonight? If I may be so indulgent as to ask."

"We're working our way through Galatians," Josiah said. "I think a little Fruit of the Spirit fits the Summertime theme. No need to make them sweat more than necessary."

Ollie laughed loudly at that. Josiah resumed the long walk to his office and the deacon fell into step beside him.

"You know, in only a few days, it will be five years since you started preaching for us." Ollie said. "Isn't that something? It seems like only yesterday."

"I'll be honest with you, I don't even remember yesterday," Joisah said. Ollie laughed again, that obnoxious tinny sound, and Josiah smiled tightly.

They stopped at his door and Josiah held out his hand with his cigar clutched between his fingers.

"Nice talking to you, deacon," he said. "I'm going to have a private little sit-down with God before the sermon. I know you understand."

"Oh yes, of course, of course." Ollie shook the reverend's hand and winced as his fingers grazed the lit cigar. "I'll be sure to leave those notes with Pollyanna," he said through gritted teeth.

Josiah winked. "Much obliged to you," he said. He pushed his office door open and slipped inside, leaving the smoldering cigar behind in the deacon's hand.

CHAPTER TWO

LITTLE FAITH

'The Oval Office' was how Josiah referred to his workspace. It was made up of a Jack-and-Jill set of rooms where he occupied both. The first room housed his desk and the built-in solid oak bookshelves where he always kept extra copies of his bestseller, 'MAKE RIGHT WITH THE ONE WHO MADE YOU'. The second room was for more personal intimations, where he offered marriage counseling and God-guided therapy for those who were in need. There was no desk in that room, just a loveseat, a coffee table, and a set of padded waiting-room style chairs.

He walked up to his desk and rolled out his leather chair to sit down. Everything was arranged neater than a pin and he never had to look hard for anything. A stack of documents separated by red tabs and labeled with sticky notes demanded his immediate attention and Josiah picked them up to start thumbing through.

The office door opened, although he didn't look up. There was only one person who would dare to walk in without knocking.

"Good evening, Rev." Pollyanna had a voice that belonged in late night chocolate bar commercials where every word came out smoother than silk. She set a glass of sweet tea down in front of him and the sides were already sweating enough to produce a ring on the desk's surface. Josiah picked up the glass and looked up at her, deliberately taking his time in sipping from the rim.

She had eyes like smoke, a steely unforgiving grey.

"Evening, Pollyanna," he said. "Did Ollie catch up with you?"

"Mhm." She produced a file from underneath her arm. "I haven't had a chance to label them, though."

"I probably won't get to look through them until tomorrow," he said. He took another sip of tea. "The studio is live broadcasting tonight and Mack wants me there early."

"Short sermon tonight, then?" Pollyanna set the file on his desk and traced her fingers over the wood. She had the long, elegant fingers of a piano player and inch-long oval nails that were as smooth as glass. She must have noticed they had his attention, because she drew them up towards her neckline and touched the tiny gold cross that was nearly obscured by the ruffles of her high-collared blouse.

Josiah sucked down a deep breath.

"A little fruit of the spirit," he said. "Nothing too deep or complicated. It's a Wednesday night, after all."

"I think you are making the right call," she reassured him. "No one wants to think too hard in the middle of the week." She moved her hand down a little lower, resting it against her stomach. His eyes followed like it was a compass arrow. "Did Mack say what he wanted?" she asked.

Josiah blinked, the spell temporarily broken, and he looked back up at her face. "No," he said, and shifted in his chair. "He just left a voicemail. But you know Mack."

"I do," she said. "Are you coming back here to get any work done, afterward?"

"Afraid not." He slouched in his chair and rotated the glass of sweet tea. "Theo would have my balls in a pickle jar."

"Hm." She lifted one leg and sat down on the edge of his desk. Pants were all the rage with modern society's women, but Pollyanna was a class act for the Lord. Her flowing black skirt gave only the suggestion of a knee, but it was enough of a tease to make his heart skip two consecutive beats.

"When are you going to marry me, Rev?" Pollyanna smoothed out her skirt, sliding her hand down her leg and drawing the fabric taut over her thigh. "The whole congregation has been asking."

Josiah's mouth went dry. He licked his lips. "Just as soon as it's legal in the state of Texas, darlin'."

She rolled her eyes. "Is that the only reason you're still shacking up with Theo?"

"Hey, now," he warned. He finished off his tea and then handed the glass back, dismissing her with a wave. "I need to finish up here."

"At least something is getting finished." She stood up. "Let me know what Mack says. Call me."

"I'll call you," he promised. She pursed her soft pink lips, as if she wanted to say something else, but she just left the room instead.

Josiah pulled into the studio parking lot at a quarter past eight, fifteen minutes later than he meant to. He got out of his Corvette and slammed the door, walking briskly through the back lot without so much as a nod in greeting towards anyone. Mack was waiting for near the edge of the set, all but puffing steam from the top of his shiny bald head.

"Josiah!" He waved his arms to flag the reverend down. "You're late! Get your ass over here and let me talk to you!"

"Cool it, Mack, church ran overtime." Josiah made a beeline for the producer, who just gave him a hard look.

"I don't give a rat's ass, we need to talk. Come into my office." Mack grabbed Josiah by his sleeve and began to steer him away even as he talked. The 'office' was more or less a broom closet with a single, swinging ceiling light that was in desperate need of a lightbulb change. Mack was too short to pull the cord, so Josiah reached up to do it for him.

"All right," Josiah said. "What is this about?"

"It's about Vietnam," the producer told him. "Your ratings are in the toilet."

"Mack, those are two different things." Josiah brushed his hand upward to bat away a floating spiderweb.

"No they ain't, not right now." Mack jabbed his finger against Josiah's chest. There was barely an inch between them so it wasn't a long journey. "Do you remember who your viewers are, Jo? Old women who want to suck on Nixon's tits and Korean War vets. And none of that pansy-ass antiwar bullshit you were spewing the other week is going to fly with them. You could hand them a load of steaming shit and tell them to clap their hands in praise and they'd do it, but not if you make yourself look like a goddamn hippie."

"Okay, okay." Josiah held up his hands. "I get it."

"Do you?" Mack poked him again.

"Yes, goddamn it! More war, less bullshit."

"No, it's *more* bullshit, *no* war." Mack pushed both sets of fingers against his temples and massaged. "I actually don't want to hear a thing come out of your mouth that doesn't involve a bunch of zeroes and the promise of prosperity."

Josiah's nose began to itch. He rubbed his wrist cuff against the tip. "I get it," he said. "Am I allowed to take a piss before we shoot?"

"Yeah, sure." Mack started to back out of the broom closet. "Get all your boom's out now before one falls out of your mouth again on camera."

Josiah's lip curled, but he didn't have a response for that one. He waited until Mack had gone before he left the closet and then made the short journey to the bathroom. He had seen the inside of nightclubs with cleaner toilets, but it wasn't his job to stay on top of the sanitation grade. Josiah locked the bathroom door and kicked down the stopper for good measure before going to the sink. He whipped out his wallet from his back pocket and opened up the billfold. Nestled between two brand new hundred-dollar bills was a small baggie with some white powder pushed into its corner. He pulled the baggie out and held it up to the light, flicking it once for good measure before opening it up.

Josiah tipped the bag over carefully and made a white line on the sink's mirror sill. He pulled out his gold credit card and scissored it down the line, cutting and then pushing the powder back into place. He rolled up one of the bills and placed it against his nostril, leaning over and going down the sill as he sucked up all the powder into his nose.

'Shit!' Josiah pulled back and snorted heavily, tweaking his nostrils as if all the powder was in danger of raining out. His heart rate kicked up and his head went light, everything around him suddenly that much brighter and that much louder.

He packed his things back into his wallet and then turned around to kick the toilet handle and make it flush. He didn't like even setting his shoe against the grimy thing, but he had to sell the illusion.

He could do this. 'More bullshit, more zeroes. Sell, sell, sell.' He bounced on his heels and clapped his hands, trying to channel that Holy

Spirit that had made him a household name for millions of God-fearing Americans.

"This is the day that the Lord has made, I will rejoice and be glad in Him!" He sang it at the top of his lungs. He stomped his foot again and again, clapping every time he smacked his heel against the slimy bathroom tile. "This is the day! *This is the da-yuh!*" He worked his jaw back and forth and came dancing out of the bathroom, flicking his wrists so that his rings caught the studio lights and sparkled like a half-dozen stars.

CHAPTER THREE

SALT OF THE EARTH

Cameras never really made him nervous. Josiah had come across his fair share of preachers who liked to demonize television and its 'corruption of the modern youth'. He was convinced that the real problem was their fear of being confronted with the big, dark lens staring them down like an all-seeing eye, plastering their stuttering lukewarm sermons across the screens of every middle-class home in America.

Not him. Josiah loved being a modern marvel in living technicolor. If television had been around in the times of Jesus, the savior would have lived to oversee his own merchandising.

And those suburban housewives and 9-5 working hour fathers needed him now more than ever. They all needed a little guidance, a few comforting words and some advice on where to send their donations. With all that excess money burning holes into their pockets, they were liable to do something asinine—such as buy a boat, or a second car. They might take a long, luxurious vacation over to Florida without thinking once about what it was costing them as far as eternity was concerned. *Soul Dollars,* that was what they wanted to rack up. *Pearly Bucks. Heavenly Hundreds.* Something like that. Those streets of gold didn't pave themselves.

The cue cards behind the camera were being handled by an intern in an oversized black t-shirt and torn jeans who blended into the fuzzy darkness beyond the glaring studio light. The cigarette smoke pouring from the white stick in Mack's mouth made Josiah's teeth itch. He wanted a cigar so badly. Still, he kept that smile plastered to his face.

"We are just going to take a moment," Josiah said to the camera. "Because I am getting a feeling right here." He balled up his fist and held it against his stomach. "God is telling me that there is someone out there listening tonight who needs a little comfort. There is someone who needs to know that God is out there listening to their prayers. Someone who is suffering from cancer of the stomach. God wants you to know that *yes*, he has heard you and *yes*, he will *heal* you." He hoped that he was reading the cue cards correctly. The intern kept pulling them in and out of his focus. If nothing else, cancer was *always* a safe bet. Josiah closed his eyes and bowed his head, holding out his hands with one still gripping the microphone as he started to pray. The choir behind him kicked up their soft, soulful version of '*He Touched Me*,' which would serve as his timer for when the prayer needed to end so the broadcast could be wrapped up.

He tried not to let his mind wander as he rattled off the words that he knew by heart, but his drug-fueled thoughts were going at a hundred miles a minute and matching his heartbeat to their pace. Every time his focus shifted his thoughts were dragged back to images of Pollyanna grinding down on his thigh. They flashed across the main screen of his brain like scenes from a drive-thru movie theatre. Her round hips, her slick, sweaty skin, her carefully sculpted black ringlets that tumbled over her soft shoulders like an old West saloon girl...

A loud buzzer sound crashed through his glowing daydreams and brought Josiah's prayer to a grinding halt. He looked up and a sharp smell flicked him in the nose—a bright, alcoholic scent that was unique to permanent markers. The buzzer ended as angrily as it began, and then the whole studio was silent. The white lights were still on, the jelly-dark eye of the camera was still focused on him, but the people were nowhere to be seen.

The cue cards rested on the ground, propped up against a stool. The closing words that were supposed to come after the prayer were ruined, like someone had taken a wet rag and swiped them down the center. The black letters ran towards the concrete floor where they pooled and then spread out in a multitude of streams. They looked like veins spread out over the back of some giant hand. They stretched all the way across the floor and came together at his loafer. They flooded around his sole and stained the sides of the white leather with stinking black ink. Something that was like revulsion, or fear, cramped his stomach and made him raise his foot from the puddle. He shook it mid-air to try and fling the ink off the sides, reaching down to wipe it away with his suit jacket sleeve. The ink did not leave, if anything he just smeared it around more. It spread over the arm of his white jacket like a bloodstain.

The cue cards rustled and then smacked against the concrete as they fell flat on their face. Josiah's head came up again as he spotted someone skulking around the edge of the stage, lingering in the darkness. He could not make out anything more than a shadow beyond the hot lights. He squinted to try and get a better look, but the figure was moving too fast.

Josiah's heart was like a lead ball being thrown against his chest. He tried to take a step forward, but the ink had gotten sticky and now it was more the consistency of tar. It held him fast, adhering him to the soundstage. His shoe might as well have been bolted to the floor.

"J-J-" He didn't even know what he was trying to say. The words were little bubbles on his tongue. They crashed against his teeth and broke apart before they could fully form. Josiah shook his head and sniffed before dropping to one knee to unlace his shoe. The shadow had completely disappeared from his vision, but the pit in his stomach had not gone away.

"J-J-Josiah," a voice, darker than blackberry tea, sauntered through the darkness and mocked his own attempt at speaking. "Found you, sweetheart."

The lights in front of him blew out and burst, filling the air with acrid smoke and raining glimmering shards of glass down onto the floor. Josiah reached up to shield his head, eyes darting wildly around every corner of the stage.

"J-Jesus!" Josiah finally spat out the word, and it took the wind out of him. "Jesus fucking Christ!"

"No," the voice said, "you get one more guess."

A hand picked up the cue cards. It was barely visible underneath the remaining lights, but Josiah caught a glimpse of ghastly red fingers ending in pointed black nails so long that they started to curve—like talons.

His whole ribcage suddenly contracted, like he was being squeezed, and he heard something crackle. Josiah hit the ground, landing face-first in the puddle of ink. It smelled like alcohol, and then like copper. It was warm, at first, then scalding hot like blood. It was filling his mouth and his nose, and it was all over his chin. It was thicker than slime, it was...

"Jo!" Mack's big hands grabbed him by the shoulders and started shaking him. Josiah choked out a half-chewed, unintelligible response that faded into a cough. Bright red specks flew from his lips and landed on Mack's face. All the producer's wrinkles came together in a dismal frown, and he whipped out his handkerchief to wipe himself clean.

"Are we still rolling?" Josiah asked hoarsely. He touched his face and his fingers came back bloody. Now that he was fully back in the moment, he could feel it gushing from his stinging nostrils.

"No, fuck no, we're not rolling," the producer said. "Because what the hell was that? Did you just stroke out on me?"

"It wasn't a stroke." Josiah shoved his sleeve against his nose to staunch the blood flow. "If we're not live, then I need to go to the bathroom and take care of this."

"Sure, whatever." Mack turned around. "Get this man some towels!" He walked away with his hands in the air. "I need a smoke!"

The same intern who had been holding the cue cards ran up to Josiah with a folded blue hand towel. Josiah nodded his appreciation and took it, pinching his nose through the fabric and tilting his head back.

The towel smelled a little bit like rubbing alcohol, but he tried not to dwell on it. Those long red fingers still crept around the back of his brain, tapping against the inside of his skull, seeking out some kind of acknowledgment that he was not ready to give.

He worked on taking that mental image and stuffing it back down along with everything else it came with. He would deal with all that later, but not now. It was not a good time.

There probably never would be.

CHAPTER FOUR

NEW WINE
OLD WINESKINS

Josiah did not go home. He sat in the parking lot of the *'Old Alamo'* motel with a box of Chinese takeout in his passenger seat and a cup of late-night gas station coffee shoved into his cupholder. The flickering neon sign above his car washed the hood out with pale shades of orange. He sucked on his teeth and ran his hand up and down the curve of the leather steering wheel, staring at nothing while simultaneously trying to think about nothing.

The key that the weaselly man at the front desk had given him glinted dully from its place on the dashboard. The look on the man's face was not one of recognition, which was completely fine by him. Josiah wasn't here to sell anymore. He had punched out for the night.

The clock on his dashboard read 10:59PM. He had spent a good deal of time driving around and trying to clear his head. It hadn't worked, that was how he ended up here. He was only forty-five minutes from home, but he was not ready for that.

He wondered if Theo had caught his little live-broadcast blip. If so, he didn't want to deal with it. And even if not, the thought of climbing into his own bed made his skin crawl.

He needed a goddamn distraction. A good one. Josiah snatched up the key from his dashboard and grabbed his coffee and his food. He balanced it all on his way to the motel door, shoving the key into the lock and giving the warped, dark green door a good kick.

The motel room was cold, and that was all he could ask for. It was musty, on top of that, and the windows were dewy, but he didn't care. Josiah set his dinner down on top of a small brown table and picked up the phone that was resting nearby. The spiral cord clattered across the table as he raised it to his ear and dialed Pollyanna's number with his free hand.

It rang three times before she picked up.

"Hello?" She sounded like she had been sleeping. Josiah licked his lips and curled the phone cord around his finger.

"Hey, Polly." He cleared his throat before continuing. "Did I wake you up?"

"Rev?" She yawned. "No," she huffed a little, her breath a crackle against the receiver. "Is something wrong?"

Josiah dragged his nails over the back of his neck. "I'm at the *Old Alamo*," he said. "Room 37. Come meet me here."

She was quiet for a moment, and he thought she might have hung up on him. Then she asked, "Is this a business meeting?"

"No," he said flatly. "Did you watch the broadcast?"

"I watch all your broadcasts," she said. "They cut it off early, though. Was that a fluke?"

He ground his teeth and pushed his nails into the nape of his neck. "I'll talk to you about it when you get here."

"Fair enough," she told him. "I need to get dressed."

"I'll wait up," he said. The line crackled again, another huffy breath or maybe she was blowing him a kiss. It went dead right after, and he held up the buzzing receiver to his ear for almost a full minute before setting it back down on its cradle.

The clock on the bedside table warned Josiah that it was almost midnight. That was when Pollyanna arrived, nearly unrecognizable in a long peach-colored coat and a devastating shade of mulberry lipstick. Her chunky platform heels made her taller than him, and when she walked through the door he caught a hint of beauty counter perfume, the perfect blend of musk and florals.

Her curls were still perfectly formed. At this point he did not know if they were just always like that, or if she had taken the time to do them before leaving home. A peachy satin bow kept the cluster of ringlets off her neck, although a few rebellious wisps refused to stay slicked down and brushed over her full, dark brows instead.

Josiah had to swallow twice before he could speak.

"You look nice," he said.

"Do I?" She turned her head to glance at him. Her curls swished with the movement. "I just sort of threw myself together on my way out." She shrugged and pulled on the belt that kept her peach coat cinched around her waist. "So, now that I am here, do I get to know what is wrong?" She prodded the empty takeout container still resting on the table. "You ate, at least."

"What makes you think something is wrong?" he asked. She raised an eyebrow and dropped the floppy peach belt, starting her fingers down the line of buttons that began at her throat.

"You told me you were going home," she said.

"I was," he admitted. "I decided not to. It was a...weird night." He sat down on the edge of the hotel bed. It was barely wide enough for a single person, much less two. He wanted to lay her out on it anyway.

"Weird how?" She kept going with her buttons. "Was it Mack?"

"Yeah," he finally admitted. It wasn't the whole truth, but he didn't see the point in talking about the incident, either. Especially when they didn't even show his bloody nose on the screen. There weren't enough hours left in the night for him to explain himself, anyway. "Mack said the ratings are going down and he wants me to ramp up the act to save us from circling the drain. Apparently, I got too political in the wrong direction."

"I did wonder how that would go over," she said. She finally dropped the peach coat from her shoulders and it fell to the floor in a shimmering heap. Underneath, the only thing she was wearing a pale blue nightdress, which was too short to be classified as anything other than obscene.

"Fuck." Josiah caught himself staring. He dragged his hand down his mouth and exhaled sharply into his palm.

"Is that why they cut you short?" Pollyanna asked. Josiah shook his head.

"Goddamn it, Polly, I don't know. I don't want to talk about work anymore," he said.

"You don't want to talk at all." Pollyanna slipped her foot out of her heel and pressed her bare toes against the edge of the bed. "You want to bury your face in my cunt."

"Yes," he said, the words coming out almost desperately. He touched her satiny calf and pressed his lips to her knee, dragging his hands down the length of her shapely leg before cupping her dainty heel. "Hallelujah amen."

She touched the top of his head, weaving her fingers through his thick black hair. "You're going to have to talk about it," she warned him, "eventually."

"Eventually," he muttered. "Not tonight." He kissed up her leg and latched onto the inside of her thigh, pausing there to suck greedily. Pollyanna moaned and leaned in closer, pushing down on the back of his head so that his face was buried in her supple flesh. Josiah could barely breathe. His nose and mouth were plugged up with her, and that was how he wanted it to be. He pushed up the skirt of her nightgown to grab a handful of her ass, squeezing tightly before wrapping his free arm around her waist and dragging her down to the bed.

Pollyanna gasped when her head hit the pillow and then moaned, sliding her hands over his scalp to travel down his back. Josiah buried his face between her breasts, grabbing them through the soft fabric and pushing them up so he could kiss them individually. He stroked her nipples through the cotton, swirling his fingers around and then pinching them, just enough to get them stiff. She groaned even louder and pulled one leg out from underneath him, wrapping it around his hip and bringing her heel to rest on the back of his thigh. Josiah ground against her hips and pushed up on her breasts again, squeezing her nipples hard enough to make her gasp. The nightgown completely failed to cover the tiny pair of panties that were barely more than a strip of color down the center of her black, curling pubic hair. Everything below his belt tightened with need at the sight.

Josiah pulled himself up just enough to undo his pants. He slid them down his thighs and revealed the white leather harness already hugging his hips over his boxers. Pollyanna's eyes widened and she squealed her excitement, bringing her legs up and grabbing hold of her knees to spread her thighs as wide apart as possible without her heels sliding off the bed.

"Oh, so you were prepared," she panted. Josiah reached over her, stealing a heady kiss as he pulled open the nightstand drawer.

"I might have tucked one in here," he admitted. "Just in case."

"Lord have mercy." It seemed like she could not stop touching him. She kept running her hands up his neck and down his back, clawing at his shirt like she could tear it off him. "Like no pastor I've ever known..."

The dildo he had brought with him was heavy and bubblegum pink. It was one of his favorites, because it was girthy but not too long, and it did not slip out of the harness. That was the most important part. He slipped it through its ring and then paused to check in on her, pressing his fingers against the hot, soaked strip of fabric that had all but disappeared inside of her.

Josiah tugged her panties aside and touched the opening underneath. She was hot to the touch and so slick that she squelched when he slipped his fingertip up and down the outside. Pollyanna moaned, and Josiah pushed deeper. He sought out her swollen, sensitive clit and began to stroke it, teasing it with short, tight circles that made her damp thighs tremble.

"Oh, Reverend," she moaned. "Oh, yes, oh, yes...fuck me, please, Reverend!"

Josiah grabbed the dildo and pressed the head against her, slipping it up and down to coat the material before sliding it in. He wanted to plunge deep inside of her. He wanted to fuck her until the bed collapsed underneath them, but he had enough restraint to allow himself to enjoy the buildup. The only way he would be able to get off, anyway, would be by seeing her thrash in ecstasy.

"Rev!" Her voice cracked. Her back arched and she dug her nails into his shoulders. Briefly, vaguely, he wished she wouldn't do that while he was wearing such a nice shirt.

"I have you," he said. "I have you." He moved his hand and rolled his hips, working the dildo inside of her while she kept her legs spread wide just for him. Pollyanna's mouth fell open, forming a little 'O' that only emitted soft whimpers. When he was hilt-deep inside, Josiah wrapped his arms around her and claimed another kiss. He pushed his tongue inside of her mouth and held her body against his while he thrust. She moaned around his tongue, welcoming it into her mouth just so she could bite down on it. He growled in return and thrust again, bracing his knees against the bed and driving himself down as deep as he could go.

Her whole body shivered and broke out into a sweat. She wrapped her legs around his hips and tightened her thighs, clinging to him as if for dear life while he fucked her. The bed shuddered and creaked dangerously underneath them, but he did not stop. Josiah pulled her up until she was nearly an inch off the bed, breaking apart from her mouth to kiss her throat and her shoulders while he thrust. She was so wet that she was gushing onto his thighs, and the dildo was gliding in and out.

Josiah pulled her up a little higher and she sat up at the same time. Josiah followed her motion and fell onto his back, holding her hips so that she could ride him comfortably.

Pollyanna was only upright for a few minutes before she was laying on top of him, locking her thighs around the dildo and sliding up and down its length, grinding down against him at the same time and moaning. He squeezed her breasts again through her nightgown, kissing her and pushing his hips up so that she could have something firm to rub against. Her weight and the friction were working him up, too. He skirted the edge of his own orgasm, but he couldn't quite get there, as much as he wanted to. Josiah growled in frustration and grabbed Pollyanna's curls, kissing her again and shoving his tongue into her mouth. She moaned around it, and her whimpers climbed higher as she rubbed against him. Finally, she tensed, and her thighs quivered as she came all over him.

Josiah broke the kiss and heaved a deep sigh. He patted her thigh and popped his hips up at the same time, signaling for her to dismount. Pollyanna groaned and slid off the dildo. It was shiny in the dim motel light and so wet that when she moved back, it sprang back towards his stomach and hurled droplets onto his shirt.

Pollyanna fell back towards the pillows and stared up at the water-stained roof. Josiah immediately stood up and tugged the dildo free from its harness, setting it down on the bedside table before heading towards the bathroom to clean up.

"Was that good for you?" Pollyanna panted. She shivered a bit as she lowered her knees and rolled over onto her side, watching him.

"Yes," he said. Josiah pulled his pants up over his wet boxers, but left the fly undone as he reached into his pocket. "How about you?"

"Wonderful," she said. He lost track of her voice as he pulled out his wallet and went fishing for the baggie that he had before.

"Glad to hear it." He opened up the baggie and poured some of the white powder onto the bathroom counter. He leaned heavily over the counter as he used a business card to cut the line. It was strange to be left so dissatisfied after being with Pollyanna, but there was a first for everything. He chalked it up to the last hurrah of what had been, overall, a bad day.

"Are you sleeping here tonight?" she asked him just as he tuned back in.

"Might as well," Josiah said. He pulled out the same hundred-dollar bill from earlier to roll up. "I have to be at the church in the morning."

CHAPTER FIVE

FRIEND AT MIDNIGHT

Sleep and cocaine did not like to tango. Josiah found himself standing outside of his motel door at three in the morning, blowing long streams of cigar smoke into the summer air and watching it drift away from his place underneath a dim yellow light.

A couple of bats fluttered around a streetlight that was only a few yards away. He watched them take turns diving for the cyclone of moths that swirled around the bulb. The portable radio by his feet played back one of his pre-recorded sermons that they liked to recycle for the late-night godless heathens.

He brought the radio with him everywhere. Sometimes, the sound of his own voice was his only solace.

Josiah took another drag from his cigar and rested his head against the textured concrete wall. Pollyanna was sleeping peacefully on the other side, tangled up in a thin hotel bedsheet and wrapped around a pair of pillows. He had left her that way and grabbed the radio from the trunk of his car.

Even with the sun fully down, it was still hotter than the devil's hellhole. Josiah wished that he could strip off his shirt, but he did not want to be caught standing around in just his binder. That was not the sort of attention he was looking for in the small hours of the morning.

The radio crackled and Josiah glanced down. The sermon became garbled, hidden behind a wash of static that was like hot grease popping in a pan. Josiah clenched the cigar butt between his teeth and squatted, picking up the radio to fiddle with the tuning knob. The static became louder, even though he had not knocked the volume dial at all. His brow knit together, and he gave the radio a hard shake, slamming his flattened palm against the side in frustration.

The sermon came back clear as a bell, but now the volume was up as loud as it could go. Josiah tried to turn it down, sweating over the idea of waking up the entire row of sleeping rooms. It did not matter which way he twisted the dial: the volume did not get any quieter. His voice continued to climb, every word of the fiery sermon punctuated by heated Southern fervor.

"AND NOW! HERE I SAY TO YOU THAT IT IS THE LORD; IT IS THE LORD WHO WILL DECIDE WHO IS HEALED TONIGHT! DO YOU FEEL IT, CHURCH? DO YOU FEEL IT DOWN IN THE TUNNELS OF YOUR CUNT? DO YOU FEEL IT SQUEEZING YOUR FLACCID GUTS? WILL YOU RECEIVE THE LORD'S FIRM ROD, JOSIAH? ARE YOU READY TO POP LIKE A FUCKING BALLOON?"

Josiah threw the radio against the wall. It smacked against the cement and then landed on its face on the concrete sidewalk, but it did not break. It crackled again, like the station was changing, and his voice distorted as it blended into something else. Something darker joined in, a voice that was like his own but pitched much lower.

"HELL-O SWEETHEART," said the voice on the radio. "DON'T YOU REMEMBER ME?"

Josiah stared at the radio on the ground. His cigar fell and he swiped his hand down the sides of his mouth, too stunned to even bend down and pick it up.

"I'm blasted," he muttered under his breath. "This isn't real." He lowered himself down to his knees and crawled over to the radio, reaching for the long antenna that jutted out from the top to pull it back towards him.

"AND THE LORD WILL BRING DOWN HIS JUDGMENT ON THOSE WHO SLANDER HIS NAME! ON THE NONBELIEVER! THE BACKSLIDER!" The voice was entirely his again. The radio scraped across the concrete as he dragged it over. He lifted it up by the antenna and mashed all the buttons on the top while trying to find the 'off' switch.

The channel switched and started playing *'Be My Baby'.* Josiah snarled through his clenched teeth and slammed his fist against the buttons, throttling the radio and doing everything short of pitching it against the wall again. He twisted the volume dial and hit the 'off' button one more time. For whatever reason, that proved to be just the ticket. The radio went quiet and he spent a good, long minute sitting on the sidewalk—listening to the sound of chirping cicadas and eighteen-wheeler trucks rolling down the nearby highway.

Maybe he needed to stop doing blow. Josiah picked up the half-finished cigar he had dropped and shredded its damp end between his fingers. The smell of tobacco was nice. It grounded him a little bit and mingled with traces of Pollyanna's scent that still lingered on his skin.

'Hello, sweetheart.' Those words buzzed around the hind part of his brain. He tried to shove them down into the same box where he kept the image of the clawed red hand and everything else associated with it, but the space was getting tight. If he ripped *that* lid off, it would all come springing free like snakes in a can. He could not afford that. He had too much work to do.

Josiah swung the radio back up to rest against his knees and pressed his thumb against one of the shiny metal knobs.

He had asked for all this, hadn't he?

The diamonds on his gold cross ring winked at him with glacial malice.

His office phone's clanging ringer was already sounding off when Josiah walked in. His hips ached and his shoulders burned from where he had not taken his binder off all night, and the last thing he wanted to see was the red light on his answering machine flashing frantically. He already had a hunch about who it was, and he doubted that it was anything really important.

Pollyanna followed him in wearing a high-collared, lemon-yellow blouse and a flowing black skirt that was long enough to brush her toes. She had, at least, thought ahead and packed some extra clothing before driving over to meet him. Her curly hair was a bit of a mess, still, but in a way he found completely darling. He liked how she looked, bedraggled and kissable yet completely untouchable, her workplace presence as rigid as a glass case around a jewel.

"Can I get you some coffee, Reverend?" she asked as she walked by him. She beat him to his own desk and picked up the little trash can beside it to empty.

"Yes, thank you," he said. Josiah sank down into his leather chair and pressed the voicemail button on his answering machine. The red light went steady as the messages played back to him.

"Hey, Rev, I don't know if you're still at the church..."

The machine beeped as he skipped to the next voicemail.

"Rev, if you could give me a call back before you..."

Beep.

"Hey, it's me again. I saw the broadcast. What the hell was that? Are you okay-?"

Beep.

"Rev. I really need you to..."

Beep.

"Josiah, I've been trying to...!"

Beep.

Josiah pushed his face into his hands and rubbed them up and down the bony ridges of his skull. He thought, briefly, about shoving his fingers into his eyeballs until they burst and ran down his cheeks. Maybe that would drive out the tension and give him something to focus on other than the pinball of stress that kept ricocheting off the spongy chambers of his heart. Theo had that effect on him. The 5,500sqft ranch-style home with an in-ground swimming pool and a kitchen bigger than most people's apartments wasn't enough. Two top-of-the-line cars redder than maraschino cherries and a church parking space with 'THEODORE WILLARD' plastered on a sign was not enough. Theo already had the best damn life that any queer living outside of Austin could hope for. Short of Heaven and Earth being moved around, Josiah wasn't sure of what he *could* do to make that man happy.

"You should call him back." Pollyanna set a Styrofoam cup down on his desk. The coffee inside was an off-putting light brown color with flecks of powdered creamer still floating on the top. Josiah made a face.

"I should make you do it," he said. "You're my secretary."

"He doesn't want to talk to me." Pollyanna folded her arms. "And he will just keep calling until you pick up."

Josiah snorted softly and picked up the coffee cup. It burned his fingertips through the sides, but he held it anyway. The stinging heat brought some clarity, a hint of pain that made his nerve endings tingle. She had a point, but that didn't mean he wouldn't rather swallow detergent.

Josiah picked up the phone and wedged it between his shoulder and his ear as he punched in the number. The other end only had the chance to chance to ring once before it was picked up.

"Hey, babe..." Josiah began. Theo cut him off.

"Do you have any idea of how worried I've been?" Theo sounded like he was near tears. Josiah rolled his eyes and sipped from the Styrofoam rim of his cup.

"Some idea." He glanced at the answering machine. "I got all your messages."

"Where were you last night?" Theo demanded. Josiah shrugged even though his boyfriend could not see him.

"I ran late at the studio," he said. "I spent the night at a motel."

"I thought you were in the *hospital!* I had to listen to some snotty receptionist tell me that if Josiah Tucker was in the emergency room, I could trust that God would take care of things," Theo said. "But what else was I supposed to think after I saw you blank-out completely on your broadcast? I mean, Christ, Jo...!"

"Easy," Josiah said.

"*Rev.*" Theo drew in a deep breath. "You looked like you were about to hit the floor. I don't even know how you're doing *now.*"

"I'm okay," Josiah said. "Last night was nothing, really. Too much..." He stopped himself from admitting what he shouldn't

52

with another sip of coffee. Theo put up with a lot, but he had made his stance on Josiah's recreational drug use clear. It didn't matter if it was pills, blow, or grass; Theo wasn't putting up with any of it. "...coffee," Josiah finally finished. "Not enough food. You know how it goes, not eating and then having all those lights shine on your face."

Theo went so quiet on the other end that Josiah thought for a moment that he had hung up. He could tell that his boyfriend didn't believe him, he just wondered if Theo was going to admit that.

"Are you coming home tonight?" Theo finally asked. Josiah exhaled slowly and set down his cup.

"I'll be back for dinner," he said. "After that I have to..."

"No, no," Theo groaned. "Come *home*. Stay *home*. I miss you. I thought you didn't have to record anything tonight."

"I *have* to drop by the studio..." Josiah argued back.

"Do you *have* to?" Theo spat into the receiver. "Or are you just looking for an excuse not to come home to me?"

"Well," Josiah growled, "you don't make it very appealing."

The other line clicked and went dead. Josiah placed the phone back on its cradle and immediately grabbed the knob of the topmost drawer on the side of his desk. His cigar box was exactly where he had left it, nestled right next to the steel cutter and the cardboard tube of long matchsticks he kept. Josiah pulled out a fresh cigar and flipped on the little blue radio that rested close to his left hand. A pleasant little gospel choir rendition of 'He Touched Me' drifted through the air and he leaned back in his chair, letting his shoulders sag to try and ease some of the tension that kept all the muscles knotted up in the middle of his back.

It was the sensation of falling that jerked him back to the moment. Josiah sat back up with a jolt and his cigar fell into his lap. It wasn't even lit.

He hadn't realized how tired he was. He grabbed his Styrofoam cup and chugged down the rest of his coffee, even though it was no longer piping hot.

It was going to be a long goddamn day.

CHAPTER SIX

GROWING SEED

Around six o'clock, Josiah pulled into his driveway and parked right behind the Buick. At least it looked like Theo was home. He wouldn't put it past his boyfriend to split and take himself halfway across town to make some sort of point. The front door was unlocked, which was odd enough to make Josiah's pulse quicken. He stepped into the house and immediately shed his suit jacket, draping it over his arm as he walked down the orange-and-red carpet runner.

"Theo?" he called out. "Are you home?" He barely got the words out before the phone's ringer interrupted him. Josiah set his teeth and walked into the kitchen, tossing his jacket over the back of a chair before picking up the avocado-green phone.

"Rev. Tucker residence," he greeted, still half-distracted by looking around for his boyfriend.

"Jo, are you still coming by the studio tonight?" From the other side, Mack sounded like he was vibrating in his seat.

"Maybe," Josiah said. "Did something happen?"

"You won't believe the ratings; they *shot up* overnight. Whatever happened to you has people calling in their sympathies and prayers and I have heard more conspiracies about the devil trying to take down God's holy shepherd in the past twelve hours than I have in fifteen years. We've got pledges pouring in."

"That's great." Josiah turned his full attention back to the conversation at hand. "I'll come in tonight. I'm at home eating dinner, but I will be there around eight."

"Suits me," Mack said. "We'll talk then."

"Bye." Josiah hung up the phone and doubled back through the kitchen. He crossed through the living room and then started down the hall. There were, honestly, far too many rooms where Theo could be sulking and he did not have time to poke his head into every single one. He started thudding his fist against doors as he walked, pausing only briefly after each knock to see if his boyfriend responded before calling out again.

"Theo!" Another heavy bang. "If you want to talk, let's talk. Otherwise, I have to get down to the studio." He stopped at the bathroom and looked down. There was a slim line of yellow light peeking out from underneath the door. Josiah flicked his tongue between his teeth and rammed his knee against the wood, following it up immediately with the fleshy side of his fist.

"Theo!" He grabbed the knob and jiggled it. It was locked. Panic tried to flutter up in his chest, but it was a murmur against a wave of calm that took over.

They had ended up here so many times, he knew more or less what he needed to do.

Josiah reached up to touch the top of the bathroom doorframe and felt around until his fingers brushed up against the metal pin he kept up there. He pulled it down and stuck it into the hole in the center of the bathroom knob. The lock clicked and he felt it spring, then he turned the knob and pushed the door open. The bathroom rug was bunched up and jammed up against the corner, but he was able to reach under and push it out of the way in order to get inside.

"Get out!" Theo screamed. "Get out, get out!"

The bath curtain had been dragged aside so violently that three of its rings had been pulled away from the rod, and its corner sagged limply against the wall. Theo sat in the bottom of the tub, where beads of water and soap bubbles were still collected on the side as if he had started to run a bath and then changed his mind. He was fully clothed in shorts and a dark tank top, but his arms were angry and red, covered in jagged lacerations where existing scar tissue had been sliced open and now the wounds leered up at Josiah like wide, gaping mouths.

There was broken ceramic in the bathroom sink. From the looks of it, Theo had slammed his favorite mug against the faucet and took the biggest piece.

Carefully, Josiah stepped across the bathroom and knelt down beside the bathtub. Swollen red trails down Theo's flushed cheeks marked the path of his tears. Josiah reached out to touch him, and his boyfriend recoiled.

"Get out!" Theo's voice was raspy. Josiah wondered how long he had been screaming, even with no one to hear him. "You don't want me, so go. Leave me here."

"I am not going to leave you here," Josiah said. He unbuttoned his sleeve cuffs and rolled them up to his elbows. He reached for Theo again, taking hold of his arm gently and inspecting the cuts. None of them were very deep this time. His suspicions about the mug were confirmed by a shard of bloody dark blue ceramic that rested on the bottom of the tub, but he did not say anything about it. He slid his hands around Theo's torso and tucked them underneath his armpits. "Stand up," Josiah said. "Lean on me."

"Why?" Theo's voice cracked again. Even though he was arguing, he did as he was told. He leaned against Josiah's chest and his blood soaked through the expensive white shirt.

"We're going to get you to bed," Josiah said. He chose his words carefully, keeping every syllable scrubbed of inflection. "Your arms need to be bandaged."

"I don't want them to be bandaged." Theo's voice caught while each breath came faster and shorter. "I just want to be alone, I am *always* alone...!"

"You're not alone," Josiah muttered. "You aren't alone. I'm here, aren't I?"

"For now," Theo sobbed.

It was only a short walk to the bedroom. Josiah set his boyfriend down on their bed and turned down the covers so that Theo could slide underneath him. Once his lover was settled, Josiah stroked his hair and asked him to stay put while he got some water. He left and came back with a plastic cup full of water and let Theo drink it down before unrolling the white medical bandages. Josiah smeared antibiotic ointment on all the cuts before wrapping them up and tucking the bandages so that they didn't unravel.

He kept the time in the back of his mind. He still had to meet Mack at the studio and now he was covered in blood. He needed a shower too, so he would probably just lock the hall bathroom door until he could get back and clean it up. He would shower in the attached bathroom and Theo could use that if he needed it. All these thoughts kept spinning around his head while he went and got Theo a second cup of water and a Valium.

"You should go." Theo shivered as he spoke. The second cup of water seemed to help him settle, and Josiah knew it wouldn't be long before the medication kicked in as well.

"I have to," Josiah said. "Mack said he needs to talk to me." He started untucking his shirt from his pants. "I'll come back afterward."

"I'm sorry, Rev." Tears welled up in Theo's eyes again. He sank down into the covers and pulled them up to his chin, peering out from over them with the saddest brown eyes that Josiah had ever seen.

"Everything is okay," Josiah sighed. He started towards the attached bathroom, already shedding his bloody clothes. "It's all going to be fine."

"I don't know," Theo sniffled. Even out of sight, Josiah could still hear him. "I don't think that I can do this anymore."

Josiah turned on the shower then paused to take in his boyfriend's words. "What do you mean?" He asked.

"I love you," Theo said. "But you leave me alone all the time and you make me feel so

terrible. I just can't do it anymore, Rev. I think
I am going to die if I stay here."

Josiah took a deep breath. He rubbed his
face and then stepped into the shower, pulling
the curtain closed. The water was way too hot.
"Can we talk about this when I get home?" he
asked, shouting to be heard above the
stream.

Theo did not respond, as far as he could tell.
Josiah wanted to feel something about what
his boyfriend had said. He tried to feel despair,
or desperation, or even anger—but all he
could feel was rushed.

Maybe after the studio, maybe after he
talked to Mack, he could feel something.
Maybe he could pull up a genuine emotion
that he could then convey to the man he had
spent the past three years with.

It wasn't like it was the first time Theo had
ever threatened to leave, either.

By the time Josiah stepped out of the
shower, his boyfriend was asleep. He grabbed
a few essentials from his drawers and a fresh
suit from its dry-cleaning bag in the closet
before stepping out to get dressed in another
room.

CHAPTER SEVEN

UNFRUITFUL FIG TREES

Rain spattered against his windshield, a little band of a wetter state's leftover storm that was sure to pass soon. Josiah kept one knee pressed against the steering wheel to keep him on course as he sped down the highway, confident in his car's ability not to go spinning into oblivion just because of some slick asphalt. He couldn't tell if it was the rain or his own exhaustion that had him seeing stars, but every time another car flew past him, his heart skipped half a beat.

Josiah drove with his knee and kept his hands free long enough to dig into his wallet and pull out the little crinkled baggie that had become his lifeline. There was just enough powder left for a bump. He poured it out onto his knuckle and sucked it up his nose, moving quickly so that he didn't lose any.

All the sudden, the rain stopped. The road stretching out in front of him was completely dry, as if the storm had skipped over it completely, while all the other cars had vanished without a trace. Without the grey clouds overhead, the sky was blood red, interrupted here and there by wisps of purple, like veins wrapped around a pumping heart.

Josiah pressed his hand against his chest, feeling his own heart thud against his fingers. The blood rushing in his ears was the only thing he could hear—louder than the wind buffeting the car as it blazed down the highway. He turned the knob on his car radio to try and break the silence, snorting hard as he did so.

"Rev," a voice crackled over the radio, partially broken-up by the static. Josiah fiddled with the knob to try and tune it, only half-focused on the highway at this point. "Rev, baby." The voice sounded like Theo's, "I can't do this anymore. I just can't. Oh my god, don't hate me. Oh my god...!"

The sound of glass breaking filled the car louder than a gunshot. It startled him so badly that Josiah's knee jerked and for half a second, he lost control of the car. Josiah grabbed onto the steering wheel and gripped it for all he was worth, making a hard swerve back into his lane and narrowly avoiding ending up in the grass or sliding along a guard rail.

His headlights bounced off something white in the middle of the road. It looked like a whole person, and they were just *standing* there. Josiah swore through his teeth and slammed his brake, veering to the side and coming to a hard halt that made his tires squeal and threw him forward. The hood of his car stopped right at the pedestrian's side. An inch to the left and he would have taken them out completely.

Josiah's head throbbed. All he could see in the rearview mirror were his own tire tracks spiraling out behind him. The pedestrian, who was now standing right beside his car, didn't even bother to move. Most of their face was obscured by his low window frame, but he was able to watch their hand as it came down towards their side and ground out a smoking cigar on his car hood.

At the same moment, he caught sight of a ring. A gold cross studded with diamonds—it was *his* ring, identical to the one he was wearing on his own finger.

The cigar smeared ash all over his cherry-red paint, and when the shock wore off, rage came to replace it. Josiah's face was hot as he struggled to open his door—although for some reason, he could not get it unlocked.

The pedestrian bent down a little and rapped their knuckles against his window. Josiah still could not see their face. He went to roll the window down, but his crank was stuck too. The pedestrian tapped again and made a gesture like they were turning a knob, then pointed inside the car. Josiah followed the line of their finger to his radio, and then he furrowed his brow, completely lost as to what they wanted him to do.

The radio was already on, so he touched the volume knob and cranked it up. A fizzle of static interrupted a commercial about Alka Seltzer, followed closely by a loud buzz that faded into the sound of someone talking.

Only it wasn't just *someone*, the voice was *his*. He hated how it sounded, although he could not put his finger on why. There had to be something off about it, but it was unmistakably him—he had watched enough of his own broadcasts to recognize himself.

"What's wrong, sweetheart?" the voice over the radio asked him. "You look like someone walked over your grave."

Josiah tried to force himself to keep taking slow, even breaths. He did not tear his eyes away from the radio, suddenly terrified to turn around and look out the window again.

"I think..." He did not even know if anyone could hear him. "I think that I am dreaming. I must have hit my head really hard."

"It's not a dream, darlin'," the voice on the radio said. "No more than it was all a dream six years ago when you came to me asking for a favor." The sound garbled a bit again, but it did not go out. "I told you then, I don't take kindly to being swindled."

Josiah's heart had not stopped racing the entire time, and now it felt like it was going to come flying out of his chest. He ground the heel of his hand against his sternum, as if that was going to force it to slow back down.

"*Swindled* is a strong word." Josiah darted his tongue across his teeth. "And if you wanted to collect your due so badly, why did you not come take it from me yourself? Aren't you devil? Didn't you bring our Lord and Savior to tears in the Garden of Gethsemane?"

The radio crackled with a loud snort. "The terms were *'come of your own will'* and *'to risk as much as you gain'.* I want it televised, babydoll. It isn't good enough for me to come like a thief in the night."

Josiah closed his eyes. "I am not going to fuck you on camera," he said. "Do you know what that would do to my career? You do, I know you do. So then, what would be the whole point?"

"Search me, honey, that's why it's called gambling. I'm not here to question your choices, I'm only here to collect." The pedestrian's hand knocked against the car window again, dragging its gold ring down the glass until it squealed. "So, what is it going to be? Your terms, or mine?"

The sound of the ring hitting the window made Josiah jump in his seat. "Go back to hell," he growled. "I am not going to ruin my life just because you made a bad deal."

His voice was on the radio again, but it was no longer speaking to him directly. This time, it was was from one of his sermons. "AND THERE IS SOMETHING THAT I MUST SAY TO YOU, CHURCH, THE DEVIL IS NOT YOUR FRIEND! SAY IT WITH ME—*THE DEVIL IS NOT MY FRIEND!*"

The pedestrian turned. Josiah could only see them from the back, but they were wearing a white suit, and he caught sight of a head of wavy black hair. His blood ran cold, like he had been jabbed through the stomach with an icicle, but he did not have enough time to over-analyze. Raindrops pelted his windshield again, a sudden downpour like God had been collecting all the rain in a bucket and just decided to dump it out onto highway. A car whizzed past him, followed by two more, and his steering wheel slipped through his fingers. It took all that for Josiah to realize that he was driving, again, and he put enough pressure on his brake to avoid crashing into the little blue car that was in front of him. Its license plate said "DAMNDIFUDO".

Josiah barely made it into his parking space at the studio. According to his watch, he was running late, so he did not take any extra time to collect himself before getting out of the car.

Mack was walking out at the same time, using the brief reprieve from the rain to try and light a cigarette while hunched over with his umbrella tucked into his elbow. Josiah cut across the sidewalk and jogged up to meet him. Mack looked up at the same time. His lips twitched and formed a hole in their left corner to release a ribbon of smoke.

"Did you forget something?" Mack asked. "The cleaning crew is still inside and can let you in."

"What?" Josiah asked. "You asked me to come out here and talk. Here I am. What did you want to talk about?"

Mack stared at him like he was crazy. The producer's brow made wrinkles all the way up his forehead, then cleared almost as quickly as they had formed. Mack tapped his nose and wiped his finger across his nostril, gesturing vaguely in Josiah's direction.

"You've got a little something there," he said. Josiah reached up and swiped at his nose. A little powder flecked away on his knuckles.

"You oughtn't do that stuff right before you start driving," Mack chuckled. He popped his cigarette back into his mouth and reached out to clap Josiah on the arm. "Get home safe, all right? See you tomorrow morning bright and early. I want you here at *9AM,* no excuses. We want that eleven to noon slot."

The smell of smoke made him feel dizzy, and his head already hurt. Josiah pressed his fingers against his temple and spread them back across the side of his skull.

His buzz was gone. He didn't know why Mack made him drive all the way out here if he wasn't going to tell him shit, but he was too pre-occupied with what had happened on the road to really linger over it.

"9AM?" he asked as Mack walked past him.

"With bells on," Mack huffed. "And nothing on your nose."

CHAPTER EIGHT

RICH FOOL

Josiah did not remember falling asleep. He woke up on his couch with a crick in his neck and one leg hanging off the side. The scratchy knit Afghan that was usually folded over the back had ended up bunched between his legs and his wand was on the floor, still plugged in somehow and buzzing against the rug. Josiah huffed and groaned as he rolled over, his shoulder burning as he picked up the wand long enough to switch it off.

His watch had ridden up his arm in his sleep and now felt like it was embedded into his flesh. Josiah moved back onto the couch and pulled his watch back down to his wrist to check the time. It left behind deep pink marks in his skin.

7:30. He needed to get up if he was supposed to be at the studio by nine.

Josiah's whole body screamed at him as he sat up. He set both legs down on the floor and had to lean over, resting his arms against his knees and taking a deep breath while he gathered up the will to make the rest of the journey. He finally pulled himself off the couch and started limping in the direction of the bedroom, dragging his right foot along while he waited for the feeling to come back to his toes.

Theo walked out of the bedroom just as he approached it. He looked up at Josiah from behind those thick glasses with pathetically sad brown eyes, then he hiked his fabric knapsack a little higher up his shoulder and tried to push his way past without a word.

"Good *morning*," Josiah said, planting his hand against the wall so that his arm barred Theo from getting by. "It's nice to see you up and moving."

"Josiah," Theo said, and his voice was soft. "I need you to let me by."

"Where are you going?" Josiah asked. He moved his arm anyway.

As soon as the barrier was removed, Theo continued to squeeze past him. "I have to get out of here," Theo said. "I can't live like this anymore. You make me feel like I'm crazy, and I am so tired of feeling that way."

"What are you talking about?" Josiah demanded. He didn't have time for this. There was *never* a good time, but Theo had a habit of picking fights during his tightest crunches. "If anyone should feel like they are going crazy around here, it's me. I don't get any sleep because I am always working to make sure that *you* are provided for-!"

"*Do not* make this about me," Theo snapped. "You were chasing your fame-driven high long before you decided to make me a part of it. Although don't worry, I don't blame you entirely. I blame myself too, for being stupid and thinking you would change."

Josiah set his teeth. "I am not trying to fight with you," he said. "I am just so goddamn tired, Theo..."

"Then stay home," Theo said. "Take a shower, get some sleep—*eat something.* When was the last time you even had a decent meal?"

"I can't stay home," Josiah said. "But we can't talk about things if you're gone. Wait until I get back." He thought about adding *please*, but that sounded too much like groveling. And he was not going to grovel, not to his boyfriend.

Theo straightened his shoulders, looking like he was holding back a sigh. "Sure, we can," he said. "Maybe I can call you and we can hash it out over the phone. I mean, we should face it. Our love has felt like a long-distance one for so long, it might feel more natural to do things that way." His expression shifted and he looked sad again, finally turning his head away. "I don't know, Josiah. Sometimes it doesn't even feel like you even *like* me that much anymore."

"Theo..." Josiah put his hand on his watch. He was tired, he was hungry, he was frustrated. His whole body hurt. His hair was greasy and his scalp itched. He felt disgusting

76

and the pain did not help his temper. His watch ticked against his hand, reminding him that time was slipping away the longer they lingered together in the hallway getting nowhere.

Theo waited for a few more seconds and, when Josiah did not add anything further, he started heading for the front door.

"Are you taking the Buick?" Josiah asked.

Theo held up his keys and jangled them. "What other car would I be taking?" he scoffed.

"That car is in my name," Josiah reminded him.

"Then call the police," Theo snapped. "I will be waiting on the headlines. *Television-Famous Reverend Calls Cops on His Secret Boyfriend—Nation Shocked by Homosexuality Scandal.*"

Josiah clenched his fist hard enough for his nails to dig into his palm and made his whole hand feel hot. He watched Theo walk out and slam the door behind him, but he did not move until he heard the sound of the car starting up.

Josiah ran to the door and pulled it open, stepping out onto the porch to watch Theo pull away. Behind his teeth, he held the words that he wanted to scream. But if he let them loose, his voice would be hoarse, and he had a broadcast to film in an hour.

It was 9AM on the dot when Josiah pulled into the studio. He would have been earlier, except he stopped to get a cup of coffee, because the crap that they put out with the stale donuts on the breakfast table wasn't going to cut it.

Five minutes later he walked through the doors, coffee in hand, feeling like death warmed over and ready to rock and roll.

"You're late," Mack said, running up to Josiah and patting the front of his white suit jacket, brushing off all kinds of imaginary lint.

"Five minutes late." Josiah slipped his blue aviator sunglasses up into his hair. "Are you going to break my balls over it, or are we going to go live?"

"You're snappy today," Mack said. "Keep it up, though." He turned away and walked off before Josiah could respond.

There was a white folding table nearby covered in donut boxes, and next to that was a large round trashcan where flies were hovering around the rim. Josiah drained the last of his coffee from its cup and tossed it into the can, stirring up the flies and sending them barreling towards the boxes for cover.

A wave of nausea swept over him. It came out of nowhere, and was strong enough that he bent over, slamming his hand down on the table and gripping its corner for dear life. Sweat broke out across his forehead and the trashcan swam in front of his vision. All those spinning black flies multiplied until they formed a mass thicker than a rain cloud. They landed on his hand and started to crawl up his arm like they were searching for something, scouting him out. Another nausea wave hit him, and it made his bowels slosh at the same time. Whatever was in there was coming out from one end or the other.

Josiah steeled himself and made a dash for the bathroom. He stayed upright just long enough to lock the door behind him and then he collapsed to his knees. The overwhelming smell of urine made him even sicker to his stomach and he lifted up the toilet lid to lean over. The toilet itself was so revolting that he had to close his eyes in order to focus on how bad he felt. His stomach gurgled and sent a gas bubble up his throat that came out as a burp, but nothing happened.

Josiah waited a few seconds and then tried to stand. Another burst of pain in his intestines dragged him back down and he moaned miserably.

It was just not his day. He would go so far as to say it was not his *week.*

Josiah put his arm against the edge of the toilet seat and leaned forward to rest his head against the crook of his elbow. He tried to focus on the way his suit jacket smelled— fresh out of dry cleaning with a spritz of cologne—but it barely helped. He closed his eyes and tried to stay as still as possible while his shoulders sagged and his whole body started caving to exhaustion. Maybe this was what happened when the body did not get enough sleep.

His stomach gurgled and he pressed his free hand against it. The pressure on his belly helped, but not enough to keep the pain at bay. His world was slowly sliding into that strange, tilting, weightless space that came right before sleep.

The last thing he wanted to do was pass out on the bathroom floor. Calling the police on Theo would have made for a shocker headline, but the Reverend Tucker waking up face-down in a toilet would have made for an unforgettable one.

He was not having much success pushing himself to his feet. There was not much distance between him and the bathroom door, so he slid away from the toilet and placed his hands against the floor. He crawled his way to the door, trying hard not to think about the grimy, slippery tile and the number it was probably doing on the knees of his white suit trousers. When he reached the door, he rose up and grabbed the handle, using it as leverage to pull himself the rest of the way to his feet. He rocked back on his heels only once. When he regained his balance, he pulled the door open.

There was an intern standing on the other side, hand poised to knock, paper badge dangling from the lanyard around his neck. He looked stunned, as if he had not expected Josiah to actually answer.

Josiah rolled his eyes and pressed his hand against his stomach again. At this rate, his only hope was to make him home before the bubbles in his stomach made their way back South.

"Tell Mack that I am going home," he said. "We can do the first morning broadcast tomorrow." He took off without waiting for a reply. With how long the intern was taking to push out *one* word, they would have been there all afternoon.

CHAPTER NINE

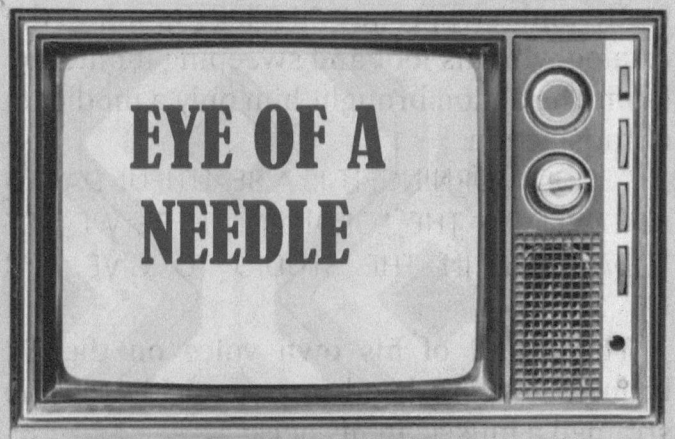

EYE OF A NEEDLE

he stomach bubbles cleared as soon as Josiah hit his couch. He stretched out and rested his head against the creaky arm, going limp with relief. He remained curled up with one hand pressed against his belly. With the other he grabbed the boxy TV remote and switched it on, pressing the cool metal plating against his hot cheek while he waited for the picture to clear.

There was an open Sears catalog resting on the coffee table. Theo had circled a few items on both pages, and they were all ridiculous things for the house. Josiah ground his back teeth and swept out his leg, tapping the catalog with his foot and sweeping it onto the floor. The action brought him only a modicum of satisfaction.

"GOOD MORNING, IT IS A BEAUTIFUL DAY TO BE LOVED BY THE LORD! AND HERE WE ARE TODAY, LIVE IN THE STUDIO TO GIVE HIM PRAISE!"

The sound of his own voice on the TV brought Josiah's head up so quickly that he strained a muscle in his neck.

"NOW, LET ME ASK YOU, ARE YOU WEARY? ARE YOU DOWNTRODDEN? DO YOU FEEL HOPELESS, LIKE YOU HAVE NOWHERE ELSE TO TURN?"

He was there on the screen, dazzling in white with the studio lights making every diamond set in his jewelry glisten like a star. His hair was combed, he wore his light blue aviators and had his cross ring-bearing hand wrapped around the hilt of a microphone.

Except it wasn't him. He was on the couch, in his own home, and what he was seeing was impossible.

He tried to look closer. Maybe Mack was upset about him running out, so he had grabbed an intern as a body double. The build was right, the voice was right, but the face would give it all away. Technology was making strides every day and even a live broadcast could be fiddled with.

The face was all out of focus. Josiah could not tell if it was the lighting or something wrong with his television. Every time the camera focused on the face; it was like trying to look through a huge smear on the lens. All the details blurred together to the point where the more he squinted, the worse it got.

That sick feeling came back like a punch to the stomach. Vomit surged up his throat and Josiah leaned over the couch to empty his guts out onto the rug. Whatever came out of his mouth looked black and it tasted like charcoal. The acid made his teeth feel like chalk. He pressed his finger against left nostril and blew, and a chunk of something came flying out.

He snorted to make sure the passage was clear, and it was almost enough to make him vomit again.

"NOW, FOLKS, I HAVE TO TELL YOU," The voice on the TV kept going. And going and going. "SOMEONE APPROACHED ME THE OTHER DAY AND THEY ASKED ME: 'REVEREND, WHAT DO YOU LOVE MOST ABOUT THE BIBLE?' AND LET ME SAY, THAT WAS THE HARDEST QUESTION THEY COULD HAVE ASKED ME. BECAUSE FOLKS, I LOVE THE BIBLE. I WISH THAT I COULD DRILL A HOLE THROUGH IT AND FUCK IT, *THAT* IS HOW MUCH I LOVE THE BIBLE."

Josiah threw up again. This time it wrenched his stomach so painfully that it brought tears to his eyes. He pressed his arm against his mouth and tried to focus on breathing. It was all spiraling out of control. This putz was ruining him on national TV and all he could do was watch it happen.

Well, maybe that wasn't the *only* thing he could do. He could go back to the studio and punch this cat's lights out. That idea was more appealing by the second.

The camera zoomed back in on the false preacher's face. Josiah found himself gaping at it while he tried to stand. His knees felt like Jell-O, and panic gripped him by the throat.

"I can't," he muttered to himself, digging his hands stubbornly into the couch beside him while trying to lift himself up. "I can't do this, Jesus..."

His knees buckled and he collapsed. His head bounced off the edge of the coffee table as he went down and knocked out all the lights.

"**R**ev?" a deep voice, like a ribbon of a dark chocolate, pulled him out of the black void and into the world where static buzzed in his ears and his head throbbed like he had been punched.

"Pollyanna?" he groaned. He opened his eyes and caught sight of her silver irises, wreathed in dark lashes and shiny like she had been crying. She was kneeling beside him, but she had pulled the corded phone down from the wall and was clutching the receiver to her chest. Her pale knuckles were the only outward sign of her anxiety.

"What-?" He gestured to the phone and started to sit up.

"You weren't responding," she told him. "I was about to call 911."

"You don't need to," he said. "I'm fine." He felt like he had been held underwater and struck repeatedly in the back of the neck, but that was beside the point.

She did not move. Josiah gave her a look and took the phone out of her hands, letting it spring back on its cord towards the wall. It just dangled there, beeping like it was swearing up a storm.

"How did you get in here?" he asked.

"You keep a key under the mat. How hard did you hit your head?" She reached out. He tried to move his head away, but she was faster. She grabbed his chin and jerked his head in her direction, pushing his dark hair away from his face so she could assess the damage.

"I don't know. Hard." He said, "I don't know how long I was out." He looked her up and down. "Why are you here?"

"I came because I saw..." Her eyes flickered towards the television. All of his rage came flooding back and Josiah leaned forward, rubbing the back of his neck.

"That wasn't me," he said. "You're going to think I sound crazy, Pollyanna, but that was *not* me on the TV."

"I am used to your crazy," she said. "What was it, then?"

"It was the devil," Josiah said, spitting out the word.

"Mhm," she nodded. "That's what the deacons think, too. Only I don't know if they see it in the same way you do." She paused and then added, "They want to have a meeting."

He wished that he was still out cold. "Of course they do," he said. "Can you tell them that I hit my head?"

"Sure, want me to say that it happened before the broadcast?" She stood and grabbed the phone at last, hauling it up by its cord and returning it to its cradle on the wall. "I think that is the only way you will get out of this one."

He thought about it. "You don't believe me, do you?" he asked. She raised an eyebrow.

"About hitting your head?" she asked.

"About the devil," he said.

"You think I don't know about the devil?" She held out her hand and he grasped it. She pulled him to his feet. "I have been Evangelical all my life. I was convinced that the devil was my math teacher in eighth grade. So much so that I wrote the principal about it. Why wouldn't I believe you?"

"That does not make me feel *less* insane," he said.

"I don't think that whether I believe you or not is the real question here," she said. "I think a *better* one would be—why is he using your face?"

"Is it not the perfect face to use?" Josiah challenged. "God's Golden Boy? The face that has been fully televised and led countless sinners to Christ?"

"Maybe." She did not sound fully convinced. "Are you telling me that that is all?"

He shrugged. "How should I know what goes through the devil's mind?" he asked. "I can only guess. Just like you."

She did not believe him. It was written all over her face. He watched her take a moment to inhale, circulating a deep breath through her nose before airing out the rest of her concerns.

"Rev," she said. "If you don't tell me the truth, I can't do anything to help you."

"You can't help me," he said. "But it doesn't matter. I don't need it."

His knees still felt too weak to hold him up. He leaned heavily against the wall with his hand pressed between his shoulder and the wood paneling. Pollyanna was wearing a different expression, now. She looked concerned. That woman could pour out a monologue with just her eyes.

He did not want help of any kind. He had taken plenty of help before, and this was where it had brought him. Except now, he was worse off than he had been, he was just crawling around in a better suit.

"In that hall closet," he said, nodding towards the hallway, "there is a crutch. It was mine. Bring it to me and I will talk to you about everything."

She did not hesitate. Pollyanna turned and made a few long strides down the hallway before finding the one door that was still closed. She opened it up and bent over, disappearing halfway into its depths. When she pulled back, she held the crutch in her hand—that hideous thing he had hoped to never need again. It was not anything special; ugly blue metal with a white cuff that wrapped around his forearm and a yellow rubber-wrapped handle that bore his weight. The scuffs on the metal were not even his fault.

Those were from the previous owner. He could not help but think of what a new one might look like—one he could have custom-made to look like gold.

An odd thought. Everyone knew that successful televangelists didn't walk around on crutches.

Pollyanna handed it over and he took it from her. The relief of having the support was corroded by his resentment for needing it at all.

"Do you want to sit on the couch?" Pollyanna asked.

"Dining room," he said. He started walking before she could say anything else. He did not want to be anywhere near the TV while he talked.

He sat down at the head of the table and Pollyanna took the chair on his right. Josiah sat in silence for a minute while he tried to gather his thoughts. They were swirling around his head so fast that it was like trying to catch fireflies with a butterfly net.

"I don't know where to start with this," he confessed. "Have you ever felt desperate? And I mean, truly downtrodden, leaving yourself open for death to come at any moment? Wishing it would?"

She searched his face with those large, silver eyes like chrome.

"Of course I have," she said. "I think everyone feels that way at least once. It is how God tests us."

That drew a weak, bitter laugh out of him. Josiah lowered his head into his hands and jammed his fingers into his hair. "If that is how God tests us, then I failed miserably," he said. "I went in the complete opposite direction of anything that God might have to offer. But I was just—so tired, Pollyanna. I was so tired of being in pain." He sat up straight again, unable to stop fidgeting.

"Were you in a lot of pain?" Her expression softened a bit, and her eyes wandered up and down his body.

Christ, he hated that look.

"Every day," he said. "There were too many days where I couldn't get out of bed. I was married to a man named Brooks. He was a postal worker, and he hated me. Always blamed me for his problems. Car broke down? My fault. Dinner was cold? He was the one who came home late, but it was still my fault. He couldn't keep his hands off sleazy magazines or his tool—always had his hand down his pants. There were so many nights when I woke up because he was jerking off next to me so hard that he shook the bed. Maybe I should be glad he never learned how to cook, with how often he was fondling himself."

Pollyanna made a face and Josiah waved his hand.

"Another life," he said. "I wasn't the same person then. At any rate, there was a church on the same road where I lived—a road called *Holden's Crossing.* Sometimes, on my better days, I could walk down there by myself. There was a night that I could not sleep and I just remember lying in bed, and all I could think about was how he *smelled* stretched out next to me. His breath was sour, and his skin seeped sweat and cum. He snored like a tractor engine, and bear in mind that I was in a lot of pain. When I turned onto one side, my hips hurt. When I turned to the other side, the pain radiated up my spine, and no matter what part of me I moved something would crackle. His snoring on top of the pain was my final straw and I just got up and left. I felt like I was going to put a pillow over his face if I didn't."

Josiah rubbed his face again. It was a part of his life he had actively tried to repress. So much good it was doing him, now. "There was light in the sky. I hadn't slept all night. I decided to take a walk out towards the church just because the path was familiar. Only, I never arrived at the church. I reached the sign that had the street name, *Holden's Crossing*, where another path crossed through mine. There was a man standing there in a red suit wearing shoes so shiny that I could see the fading stars reflected in the tops."

"Was he the devil?" Pollyanna asked. "Did you know if he was?"

"I knew. I don't know how I did; I just had a feeling like he was the answer to all my problems. He pulled all my desires out of me like they were on the end of a string. I told him everything I wanted. I wanted success. I wanted fame. I wanted to walk without pain. I wanted to be seen and treated as a man, no matter what it took. It all came out with spit and blood and then I was just a sobbing mess in the dirt. It was pathetic, really."

Pollyanna reached out across the table, offering her hand again in a different way. This time, he did not take it.

"And just like that, he was willing to give it all to you?" she asked.

"Not quite like that. He told me to narrow my focus," Josiah said. "He picked me up and dusted me off and told me to have some goddamn pride. He said it's all money—money gets you anything you want. Image, respect, medical treatments, fame. He painted a beautiful picture and he told me that if I paid him his due then I would get it all."

"And his due was...?" Pollyanna prompted.

Josiah shifted his back teeth. "He said that I had to be willing to 'risk as much as I gained', and that it would come 'as a pound of flesh'. I thought, well, I've slept with worse. He told me to seek him out when I had what I was reaching for."

"But you didn't," she concluded. "You never went looking."

"Part of it was that I always felt I could achieve a little higher," Josiah said. "And as the years went on without consequence, and as I became busier, it became easier to neglect the idea that the devil might come after what he was owed."

"But now he has." She shook her head. He could tell that there was a question lingering on the tip of her tongue, but she was holding it back for some reason.

"Go ahead," he said. "You might as well ask me what is on your mind, now."

"Why a preacher?" she asked. "That is what I can't figure out."

He thought about lying, but there was no point. He had told her this much. Although the truth of his career choice seemed somehow less believable than an infernal bargain.

"I always wanted to be one," Josiah said after a minute. "When I was young, before my life became so complicated. I don't think I need to tell you all the reasons why it would not have worked out in my favor. And sure, now it's all business at the end of the day, and the only person I haven't convinced fully of God's love is myself. I don't buy the shit that I am selling from behind that pulpit or in front of that camera, but there was always a part of me—maybe the same part of me that married that idiot—that had enough conviction to make it authentic."

It was different, now. She thought he had been one thing, and now she knew a different story. It was his turn to do the pitying.

"You don't have to stay with me," he told her. "Theo already jumped ship."

"I am going to think about it," she said. "We have to get you down to the church so you can talk to the deacons. I'll drive."

"Like hell," he said, already grabbing his crutch. "We're taking the Corvette, so I'm driving."

CHAPTER TEN

THE
WEEDS

The Corvette's windshield was cracked. That was the first thing that Josiah noticed. A gummy yellow residue had collected in the spiderweb-thin lines and broken white eggshells tumbled down the hood. Eggs alone couldn't have done that kind of damage, even when hurled from a distance, but the offending weapon was nowhere in sight. The whole passenger side had been keyed. The words "FALSE PROPHET" were etched into the red paint so deep that the metal underneath peeked through.

Josiah's blood started to run hot. It shot up his neck and flooded his face, making him feel red all the way to his ears. He was gripping the crutch so hard that his sweaty palm ached.

'The devil gave it. The devil took it away,' he thought.

Six years of toil were going up in smoke faster than he could pull himself together.

"We'll take my car," Pollyanna redirected him. Her car was a white Thunderbird and the interior was red leather. Her windshield was in one piece, but she had not been spared the furious hail of eggs. Nor had her driver's side doors been overlooked. The word "WHORE" had been scratched into the paint, but the color made it less visible.

"Give me your keys," Josiah said. Pollyanna did not argue with him. She relinquished them and slid into the passenger side. Josiah tossed his crutch into the backseat and grabbed the steering wheel, which was hot enough from being the sun coming through the windshield that he hissed through his teeth.

"Are you sure you're up for this?" she asked.

"Damn sure," he said. "We will be making a stop first. Whatever the deacons have to say to say to me, I will not be on the receiving end sober."

Hell's Belles was not the sort of joint that you rolled up to unless you knew somebody, or you *were* somebody. It was nearly an hour drive in the opposite direction of the church, hidden down through a tunnel of trees at the end of a long dirt road with no entrance sign. Josiah liked it there because they believed in anonymity. The other patrons never treated him like his face was on billboards, if they even looked in his direction.

He had only ever spoken with two people, the person who watched the door, and the boss. He had never made it past the first level, either. He knew of a rumor that the club went down for several floors, but they were more exclusive—open only for levels of clearance or cash he didn't have.

He could almost taste Pollyanna's apprehension as they pulled up. He had to check in and hand over her keys to a valet. There was nowhere visible to park.

"Rev," she said. "This doesn't feel like a good place."

"It isn't," he said. "But it's the only place where you can get the good stuff. And I mean the *very good* stuff."

Her body visibly stiffened and she raised her chin. If she was putting on a brave air, she was wasting her energy but he wasn't going to tell her that.

The club had orange and red patterned carpets and the walls were blood red, also. The gold-tinted, hazy air swallowed them up as soon as they stepped through the entrance. It smelled like smoke and Butterscotch Schnapps, which oddly enough was Pollyanna's favorite. Josiah only knew that because he had tempted her to drink, once, the first time they were alone together. They sat on the roof of the *Old Alamo* and split the bottle while the streetlights flickered and other couples, less repressed than they were at the time, fucked loudly in the rooms below.

The same night as the first really, really bad fight he ever had with Theo.

Josiah brushed that memory as far back as he could and sat down at the bar, resting his crutch against the underside and hoping it didn't slide over.

Pollyanna did not have it all figured out, but she still believed in God. Bringing her into the one place where Josiah finally felt some peace from God's relentless judgment was probably not his most endearing move.

She was silent as she slid into the stool next to him. Josiah rested his hand on her leg underneath the bar.

"Well, well. Hello, sunshine." The all-too familiar voice drifted from behind the counter, preceding its owner by only a few seconds. It came slithering in on a tongue of thick gray smoke, streaming from the burning orange end of a cigar. A hand came up and grabbed the cigar, flicking its end so that it scattered orange sparks that reflected off a pair of round lavender lenses.

"Hey, Bee," Josiah breathed. Bee was like a saint to him in these trying times, but he did not know of anyone else who would describe the club owner that way. He was the type who a three-piece suit regardless of the weather, but his shirt was almost always unbuttoned, and his sun-soaked chest was covered in a vast field of curly dark hair. He didn't look like there was much to him, no more dangerous than your average used car salesman, but there was something behind his eyes that promised a lot more if you dared to look close enough. Josiah never did. He had enough trouble in his life. Bee always kept those dangerous eyes covered with a pair of round shades, but they were never dark enough to take away from the piercing blue color.

"Are you here for a little devil's dust?" Bee turned his head and glanced at Pollyanna. His smile widened, enough to flash his gold fang. "Enough for two? Cute dates don't get you a discount."

"I don't do that sort of thing," Pollyanna retaliated. She was braver than Josiah, for that.

Bee laughed. "Sure don't," he said. "That's not what gets your engine revved, is it, Ms. Whiting?"

Josiah felt her hand grip his underneath the counter.

He wished that Bee wouldn't do this, not with her. But until he had that bag in his hands, Josiah was not going to start bucking.

"Do I know you?" Pollyanna asked.

"Nope," Bee said. He picked up a shot glass and spun it around in his fingers with lazy expertise. "I'll take a humble guess." He pulled out a bottle of Irish Whiskey and filled the shot glass almost to the top. Then he added a splash of Butterscotch Schnapps and filled a second shot glass with orange juice before sliding both across the bar counter. He pointed at the alcohol first, then the other. "Drink, then chase," he ordered.

Pollyanna did as she was told. Her obedience was as quick as lightning without a second of hesitation behind it. She knocked back the liquor in a single swallow and then chased it with the orange juice. A little shiver of ecstasy escaped her lips, and Josiah clenched his thighs.

"Good girl," Bee said. He leaned against the counter and pulled out a black playing card from his sleeve. "Are you sure that you won't indulge?"

"No, thank you," she said, still a bit breathless. Her lips were ruddy and her eyes were a little bit brighter than before. Josiah was suddenly very aware of her rapid, beating jugular and her soft, warm skin stretched over her bare throat. He wanted to launch himself from the stool and pull her body close to his. He wanted to kiss her, to tear her apart with his teeth.

He stayed seated, but only because he kept the toes of his shoes hooked around the barstool legs.

Bee shrugged. He swept the edge of his card across the bar and a thick white line, thicker than Josiah ever poured for himself, formed in its wake. On the second swipe, he scissored the card over the line, staggering little clefts of separation.

"Here you are, Preach." Bee passed over a silver straw. Josiah's fingers twitched before he even reached for it. "Are you taking some to-go?"

"As much as you can give me." Josiah put his head down and focused on sucking up every last bit of the line in front of him. When he was finished, he ran his finger over the counter and sucked the remnants off his own skin.

The rush was worth waiting for. Suddenly, his mind was clear. Josiah closed his eyes and praised God under his breath, clenching his fist against his thigh and trying not to act a fool in front of his dealer.

"I'll put it on your tab." Bee darted another glance towards Pollyanna. "Another shot for you, sweetie? On the house."

"I don't think that I should." She looked like she wanted to, with her fingers curling and uncurling against the counter like a cat flexing its claws. "Do you know about Rev's problem?"

"Pollyanna," Josiah snapped. "That's enough."

"Josiah Tucker has a problem?" Bee raised his eyebrows. It did not come across as innocent as he probably thought it did. "I thought he was living a little too high on the hog to have those."

"Not nearly." She drummed her fingernails against the counter. "I think I'll take a second shot after all."

"Pollyanna..." Josiah sniffed and tweaked his nostrils. He couldn't tell if his ears were ringing or if his heart was just beating so fast that all he could hear was the rush. All the colors in the room were starting to blend together. They didn't have time for this.

She shot him a look. "We can't leave until I'm ready to go, right?" she asked. "I don't think I want to be sober in front of the deacons, either."

Bee was already pouring the Irish Whiskey. "Preach, how about a nice Whiskey Soda? I think that will mellow you out."

"Sure," Josiah said, only half-thinking about it. He watched Pollyanna knock her second shot back like it was water. He couldn't decipher what he was feeling, only that it was something close to panic. Like if Bee found out that his career was falling to pieces, he would think that Josiah couldn't pay for his blow. "It's not really all that serious."

"Nothing ever is," Bee responded. "You like to make mountains out of molehills." He placed a glass in front of Josiah and those bright blue eyes blazed like cold fire from behind their purple lenses. "I saw your sermon this morning, Preach. It was damn funny. Maybe your best."

Josiah was too taken aback by the first half of the statement to be insulted by the latter. "You watch my sermons?" he asked.

"'Course I do," Bee said. "I've always had a thing for puppetry."

Josiah wasn't sure what that meant, and his head hurt too much to try and figure it out. The bubbly Scotch on his tongue was too refined a flavor profile for his coke-dulled palette, but it was at least refreshing.

In his peripheral vision, Pollyanna took another shot.

"What's this problem that you're having?" Bee asked. He had a way of framing things that made it sound like he genuinely cared. Josiah knew that he didn't—that bartenders and club owners just knew what to say to keep you racking up your tab. At the same time, he didn't care. Maybe it was the coke, maybe it was the Scotch. Being used in even the most passive sense felt good.

"I sold my soul," Josiah said. He didn't mean to tell the truth; it just came out of him like a loose thread being pulled from a seam. "I don't know how to get it back."

Bee flashed him a wide smile without a flicker of mirth behind it.

"No getting it back," he said. "Who did you sell it to?"

Josiah scrunched up his brow and took another long sip of his drink.

"The devil," he said.

"Be more specific," Bee urged.

"Didn't think it got more specific than that." Josiah glanced over at Pollyanna. She was not paying attention to the conversation. She was running her candy-red tongue along the inside of the shot glass and gathering up every last bit of residue she could taste. She used her tongue to draw the glass closer until she wrapped her lips around the mouth and the tip of her tongue flickered over the bottom.

There was nothing in the world between her and that last unobtainable drop.

"There must have been something that he gave you." Bee was starting to sound annoyed. "Think back on it."

"The devil has many names," Josiah argued back. "Lucifer, Satan, Beelzebub..."

"Stop it," Bee snapped. His face went dark like a switch had been hit, every trace of levity suddenly erased. He reached up and pinched the edge of his sunglasses, adjusting them on his nose as if it took every inch of restraint not to rip them off his face.

Josiah swallowed. He touched his own throat, and his modestly formed Adam's Apple bobbed underneath his fingers.

"Holden," Josiah said, thinking back to the street where the bargain had been struck and the bold black words printed on a white sheet of metal. That was the only other thing he had, and he hoped it was good enough.

His long, wavy locks stuck to the back of his neck. He was sweating so much and his heart was racing so fast. He was going to have a heart attack here, he was sure of it. He wanted Bee to look away. He thought about asking for another drink just to give the bartender something else to focus on, but he could not bring himself to do anything other than squeeze the half-empty glass in front of him.

After what seemed like an eternity, Bee smiled again, flashing his gold canine and sliding a fresh Whiskey Soda across the counter.

"Don't worry," Bee said. "Most of it's the drugs."

Josiah didn't know what *'it'* was supposed to mean, but he accepted it and chugged down his new drink.

"This devil of yours sounds like nasty work," Bee said. "He's certainly got you wound up nice and tight. But you ought to know something: time is a malleable thing. It only exists as far as that ticking watch tells you that it does. It can only be used against you because you believe it's a finite source, something you can run out of." He flashed his tongue across his teeth. "Catch my drift?"

"No," Josiah said. He pushed his hand through his hair. The short wisps that made up his curtain bangs were so sticky.

"You wouldn't," Bee said. "That's as much as I can boil it down for you, sugar, but I want you to hear me on this. Your devil is impatient, and he likes to get what he wants *exactly* when he wants it, if not sooner. But he can be forgiving, more forgiving than Jesus. And he's not above letting you take a second shot at something. So, when you walk out that door, you may find yourself taking a few steps back. Try not to get in your head about it, and remember that nothing ever plays out the same way twice."

Josiah stared down into his glass. He could barely see the counter through the thick bottom where a few bubbles still clung. It looked like a face peering up at him, and the longer he looked, the more alive it seemed.

'Most of it's the drugs,' Bee had said. Josiah went to rub his face again and accidentally smacked the glass against his brow.

Bee laughed. "I think you've had enough." He set a slip of paper down in front of Pollyanna and handed her a sleek gold pen. The ink that spit out her signature was bright red underneath the bar lights.

"It's mine," Josiah said in protest. "I'll take care of it."

Bee pried his fingers off the glass and took it away from him, replacing it with a tightly twisted baggie of white powder.

"It's all right, Preach," Bee said. "When you're as rich as you are, you never really pay for anything."

CHAPTER ELEVEN

PRICELESS VALUE

Josiah pulled his head up from the sink and glanced at himself in the mirror. Bloodshot eyes, dark circles, and a sore on his bottom lip from where he had singed it with a lighter. Water dripped down his face, sliding off the tip of his nose and disappearing off the ledge of his chin. His diamond-studded cross earring dangled from one soft lobe, and he wondered what would happen if the back snapped off and it came free. He pictured it vanishing down the tarnished, gaping sink drain and then looked at himself again. He ran his hand over his rough jawline—stubbly, but overall shaved. Hadn't he just been growing out his beard?

Josiah rolled his shoulders to try and shake off the strange feeling that crawled up his spine and grimaced at the mirror, sweeping his tongue over his teeth.

He tasted blood. He leaned in closer and bared his teeth at the mirror. There was a rust-colored coating on the enamel, and even more blood crusted in the groove above his lip.

He must have smacked himself in the face, somehow. His head hurt. There was a small glass bottle of mouthwash sitting on the sink and he grabbed it, tipping the gasoline-colored liquid into his mouth.

It burned like hell as soon as it touched the inside of his injured mouth. Josiah spat it all out almost as quickly as he welcomed it, grimacing and filling his palm with water to chase the rest of the taste out.

The taste of alcohol brought him back. Although back to *where,* he was not sure. The sink was not his. He was jammed into some tiny, yellow-tiled bathroom that smelled like roach-killer and piss. When Josiah opened the door, he stepped out into a motel room where the air conditioner left condensation on the dirty beige walls and the carpet squished under his feet as he walked.

The *Old Alamo.* He tried to remember what he was doing before he came here, but his brain was too fuzzy. Every time he tried to formulate a thought it made his temples pound. Josiah looked around the room to collect clues, but all he saw was his Bible on the table and his blue aviator sunglasses. There was not a suitcase in sight.

Josiah's eyes flickered over to the corner where a small breakfast table had been shoved into an odd nook. A blue metal crutch was propped up against it.

His heart skipped a beat. What was *that* doing here?

Pollyanna. The name rang through his consciousness like an alarm. Josiah flicked his wrist to check his watch, but it had stopped ticking.

What day was it? Josiah flung himself down onto the hard edge of his bed and grabbed the motel phone. He started to dial out, and then paused, glancing at the door.

He remembered this room. He remembered calling Pollyanna and asking her to come to him.

But that had been days ago.

Hadn't it?

He finished dialing her number and continued to watch the door as the phone rang. It kept ringing and ringing until her answering machine picked up. Josiah didn't bother leaving a message. He just hung up and stood, grabbing his keys.

He glanced at the crutch, and then he grabbed that too. He shoved his keys into his pocket and walked out of the motel room.

It was an oven-door-air type of hot. A series of dim, sickly yellow lights dotting the doorways of each numbered room collected spiders and moths all the way down the sidewalk to the office. Josiah could barely see his Corvette, but it was there. The relief that hit him when he realized it was in one piece was so big that it was almost nauseating. His knees shook a little bit, and he leaned with his hand against the hood to steady himself. He did not know, or remember, what it was that he expected to see. He only had a gut feeling that something had happened, but she was okay.

Josiah gripped the handle of his crutch and glanced back at the room he had just left. The brass number 37 nailed to the front of the door was corroded green, but it was important somehow.

It was more than a playful little sense of déjà vu. Either he was going crazy, or he had really been rolling and now he was trying to piece together exactly how he had gotten himself here. *Again.*

He walked around the side of his car and pulled out his keys to pop open his trunk. There was not much inside except for the black shoulder-bag he kept his strap-on in and his portable radio. He grabbed the radio and flipped it around to take a look at all the buttons and dials on the front.

The radio itself looked like it had taken a beating. The plastic and metal were scarred like it had been dragged across concrete.

Clarity hit him like a freight train at the sight of the radio. Everything came clamoring back. The voice, the impersonator, the dark club where he had drunk too much and snorted half his paycheck. Bee had said something to him in that place about time, and now, somehow, time had been walked back. Josiah did not know how it was done, but he remembered very clearly the words *'nothing ever plays out the same way twice'.*

Maybe that was true. His shaved face made more sense to him, now. Some things were just going to be different.

He could handle that.

Josiah turned on the radio and fiddled with the volume and tuning dials. The radio let out a high, electrical whining that cross-faded into a static hum, and somewhere underneath it he began to pick up the sound of a gospel choir.

Josiah held his breath. He kept turning the knobs, watching the needle behind its narrow glass window shiver as it zipped up and down. He was so transfixed by its journey that when a voice came through the speakers, it startled him so badly that he nearly dropped the whole device.

"HELL-O, SWEETHEART," the voice could have been his, but it was distorted and pitched lower than he could ever drop. "GOOD TO SEE WE'RE BACK ON SPEAKING TERMS."

Josiah's mouth went dry. He sat down on the edge of his open trunk and held the radio in his hands, staring at it like it was going to form teeth and a tongue in front of him.

"I know what this is about," he said. He squeezed the sides of the radio until he heard plastic squeal. "You want your due. You've come to collect."

"BEEN THINKING REAL HARD ABOUT IT, HAVEN'T YOU?" The voice on the radio crackled, but the snark was evident.

"All this because you want me to fuck you on Live TV." Josiah's voice cracked a bit as he said it. "Seems like a lot of effort. What is the point?"

"IT'S A RUSH, ISN'T IT? LOSING EVERYTHING ONLY TO GAIN IT ALL BACK IS A HIGH YOU WON'T BE ABLE TO CHASE TWICE. AND YOU LIKE THRILLS, DON'T YOU, BABY?" The dials twisted on their own underneath his thumbs, the metal grooves moving against the grain of his fingerprints. The voice became clearer, and it sounded even more like him. "OF COURSE YOU DO. YOU WOULDN'T HAVE GOTTEN THIS FAR OTHERWISE."

"This isn't some cheap thrill." Josiah ground his teeth so hard they drove pain into his gums. "This is my *life*. This is everything I have worked for!" He was close to shouting in the parking lot, still sitting on the edge of his trunk and gripping the radio tight enough to make his hands numb. He probably looked like a maniac.

"A LIFETIME SUMMED UP IN SIX MEASLY YEARS? MY, AIN'T THAT SAD? DO YOU KNOW WHAT SIX YEARS IS TO ME, SWEETHEART?"

"Fuck you!"

"I'VE TAKEN SHITS THAT HAVE LASTED LONGER THAN YOUR SIX YEARS."

His anger swelled in the form of tears. Josiah could not stop them once they began collecting behind his lids. He let them flow and watched them splatter against the radio, fighting his own agony to keep a wail from clawing its way out of his tight, burning throat. Every sound he made came out tense and ragged, every breath like a bread knife being dragged down the side of a cutting board.

"Why give it to me," he wondered aloud, "if you were just going to take it away?"

"WHY ASK FOR IT AT ALL?"

Josiah found himself looking upward at the sky. He wanted to see stars, but there was only the hazy glow of light pollution. Too bright to offer sleep, too dark to walk around in. The paralyzed face of a timepiece frozen between night and day.

Hell, he thought, and any place outside of time had to be entirely without stars.

"It will not end if I don't allow it," he said, finally. The radio crackled in his hands, as if the devil was getting excited.

Josiah slid off the edge of his trunk and stood. He sniffed to dry out the rest of his unshed tears, snorting and spitting onto the sidewalk before slamming the trunk shut.

"It will not end." He repeated it under his breath like a mantra. "It will not end." He swung the radio up by its handle and looked at the dials like he was staring the devil in the eyes. "I have come too far."

"IS THE SKY FALLING, BABY DOLL?" The voice still sounded far too much like his.

"Where do you want me to meet you?" Josiah growled. His heart was pumping far too fast. Buckets of blood in his face, his hands, his groin.

"JUST SHOW UP TO WORK LIKE A GOOD LITTLE BOY. I'LL BE THERE," the devil said.

"I bet you will be," Josiah said.

No sooner had the words left his mouth that the radio switched back to a Southern Gospel quartet. They were right in the middle of '*Ride That Glory Train*'. Josiah thought about hurling the radio across the parking lot, but he did not want it to fly into the highway.

Instead, he held onto it as he walked back into his motel room. He briefly considered trying to get a little sleep while he could before returning home, but as soon as he stepped over the threshold his exhaustion vanished and was replaced by a heady anxiety. There was no way he was going to get any sort of rest.

He did a bump instead, even though his nerves were shot, and then picked up his things before getting back into his car.

CHAPTER TWELVE

CASTING OF THE NET

The cold air coming out of his car vents as he flew down the highway was sickly sweet with a sharp, clear undertone. Like Butterscotch Schnapps. Josiah rolled down his windows to let fresh air circulate instead as he applied even more pressure to the gas pedal, watching the needle on his speedometer creep closer and closer to the '100' embedded in his dashboard. He kept the radio turned off, grateful for the silence just this once. Usually, he couldn't stand it. The only sound came from the wind as it sputtered past his open window, creating a dull roar that was easy enough to ignore but present enough to keep those loose fragments of his mind from flying in twenty directions at once.

He kept his eyes on the road and his focus on getting home. It took every ounce of his concentration to do even that much. The darkness was suffocating, and his sad little yellow headlights were not cutting the mustard. The faded marks on the asphalt were his only hint that he was even on the correct side of the road.

Black tire tracks appeared like smudges of ink. They blazed through the thick white line that ran along the side of the road and disappeared into the grass. Josiah was so caught up in following them that he almost veered off the road and ended up in the same spot. He grabbed his steering wheel and caught his breath at the same time, choking on his own panicked inhale as he veered back onto the highway. When he turned, his headlights glanced off the side of a brilliant white Thunderbird, and he only got a few feet down the road before he braked hard enough that his head went snapping forward.

There was no one behind him. Josiah popped open his glovebox and dug around until he found a small flashlight. The pale beam did even less than his headlights when it came to parting the darkness, but the Thunderbird's headlights were bright, and the front was smashed so far inward that the car itself looked cross-eyed. The engine smoked like a dragon, or some other mythological beast, and belched coal-colored clouds into the atmosphere enough to create a smog.

It rested, impaled, on the end of a steel railing. The rail had punched right through the grille and taken a good deal of the hood's paint with it.

What looked like hundreds of deep cracks spiderwebbed across the windshield. Josiah's heart pounded in his throat. He could feel the fearful throbbing on the back of his tongue. Any rush he had from the drugs was gone. He was cold-stone sober and staring at the totaled car like it was an open casket.

He did not want to point his flashlight towards the driver's seat. He did not want to know who was behind the wheel. There were so many white Thunderbirds on the highways of East Texas. What were the odds that it could be...?"

Josiah gripped the flashlight a little tighter. He held the beam on the driver's side door, creating a solid white circle of impossibly bright light. If he stared at it long enough, maybe he would go blind.

He began to move closer. On his second step, Josiah found himself muttering. He wasn't sure if it was a prayer or just crazed jabbering. It wasn't like God was listening either way, if God was even something more than a face worn by devils, acting as a shiny lure.

The driver's side door was hanging partly open. Josiah grabbed the side and closed his eyes.

"Lord, don't let this be her." He drew in a deep breath. Josiah yanked the door open and shined his light on the interior.

Pollyanna was slumped over in her seat, her peach-colored coat and her made-up face completely covered in blood. She had one hand still barely clinging to the wheel, and there was so much glass embedded in the soft webbing between her fingers that it looked like she had begun to crystallize. Most of the blood was streaming down from a nasty gash near her hairline. The skin had peeled back far enough, and heavily enough, that white bone was visible at a glance. There were still a few strands of hair attached to the torn flap, and they fell clumsily over her face.

A violent surge of acid shot up his throat. Josiah turned his head and reached out to hold the side of the car as he puked into the grass. As soon as he doubled over, everything rose to his mouth and started pouring out like a rain-filled gutter. If he hadn't been sober before, he was now.

Josiah's legs shook. He had not thought about grabbing his crutch before leaving the car and he was regretting it, now. He fought the urge to sink down to his knees. The last thing he needed was vomit and grass stains on his suit. All he could think about was the dry-cleaning bill that would rack up.

Dry-cleaning was an odd thing to think about, but it was better than thinking about Pollyanna's head being split open like an overly ripe watermelon. The smoke and the blood both left the taste of metal on the inside of his mouth. Josiah retched into the grass again and spit.

"Turn your radio on." Pollyanna's resonant contralto drifted through the air. It was softer

and more strained than he remembered, like there was a hand squeezing her by the throat as she struggled to sing. Which was impossible, of course, because no one else was on the road. *'Doubly impossible, because Pollyanna is dead.'*

Josiah glanced over his shoulder to make sure he was right in that assumption. He couldn't bear to bring himself to look inside the car again, but he caught a glimpse of her long white leg and that was enough. Josiah turned his head back around, swallowing down another cresting wave of nausea.

"Get in touch with God." Pollyanna's voice became garbled. *"Turn your radio on..."*

A pale foot appeared, and then another— turned grey with loose dirt and dark blades of grass that had become adhered to the tops. One leg was bent out at a wicked angle and the attached foot was holding its distribution of weight on its side, while mottled bruises climbed up both shins before disappearing behind the hem of a peach coat. Josiah's eyes continued to climb until he settled on Pollyanna's face, reduced to nothing but silver eyes peering out through a red, bloody mask.

She was behind him, dead, in the car. And somehow, she was standing in front of him, too.

There was a fear behind her eyes that he had never seen before. Pollyanna looked right through him like she was reading the writing on her own tombstone. Her mouth still hung open, even though she was not singing anymore. And for a moment, it looked like she was inhaling the engine smoke.

Except, no, the smoke was coming from her mouth. Pollyanna's throat visibly convulsed as she gagged, coughing up more smoke while her shoulders shook and her hands spasmed at her sides. Her mouth became a black hole in the center of her face. No lips, no teeth, no tongue at all—only absolute darkness.

Something bright and orange flickered at the back of her throat. Josiah held onto the side of the car like he was in danger of being swept up by an act of God. He could not look away. He watched the orange circle get bigger, and then something tanned and fleshy followed. It took Josiah a moment to realize that it was a hand, a *whole* hand, and it was traveling up through Pollyanna's esophagus like she was a puppet.

The hand came out to rest right where her teeth should have been. It had a thick cigar clutched between its beringed fingers, and the cigar was putting off the same foul, black smoke as the Thunderbird's engine.

"I told you that you didn't have to pay, Preach." The darkness pulled itself back for Bee like a stage curtain and he appeared beside Pollyanna, his arm bent like his hand was the one jammed into her mouth. "Your tab was picked up."

"I don't..." Josiah could not take his eyes off Pollyanna and the way she was just hanging from Bee's arm like meat on a hook. "Is it you?"

One of Bee's arched brows sprang up and he laughed. It might have been a laugh. He sounded like an excited hyena.

"No, fuck no," Bee said. He pulled his hand around to stick the cigar in his mouth, dragging Pollyanna along at the same time. "I don't want your soul, Josiah Tucker, it smells like wet pennies."

"She didn't deserve that." Josiah wanted to look behind him again. Maybe if he saw her body again, he could convince himself that he was hallucinating all this. "She didn't do a damn thing to you. It wasn't supposed to go this way."

"It didn't," Bee said. "Until it did. That's what you get, sometimes, when you rewind the clock even by a little."

"You knew." There was so much blood on the grass where Pollyanna, or whatever version of her Bee had his claws inside, was standing. "You could have at least offered me a choice."

"Come off it," Bee snorted, no longer sounded amused. "Like you would have chosen differently? This is your career, Preach! You're the golden ticket to Heaven for every willing sheep. And don't look so demoralized, there's always another broad." He shook his arm and Pollyanna let out a pained, muffled whine. "See? She agrees. Anyway, you got your second chance. Are you going to waste it standing there, looking like an idiot?"

Josiah swallowed hard while trying to keep his pride in his mouth. He had seen dead bodies before. He could not count how many funeral sermons he had preached. He had seen his own uncle whiter than wax and dead from a brain tumor, with liver spots all over his shiny head and his mouth twisted like silly putty into a smile that did not look like his at all.

But he had never seen Pollyanna dead. He could still feel her skin against his, and she had been so warm. She wore perfume from a pretty bottle he had gifted her one Christmas, and she wore a smile in the corner of her mouth just for him.

She had looked him up and down in her secret, cunning way. Like she did the night they drank on the motel roof. She admitted to him there that she had hunted him from the start. When he brought up Theo for the first time, her only response was a question: *'What has that got to do with me?'*

She was not warm anymore. There was too much blood for him to smell her perfume.

"You didn't love her." Bee's words cut into Josiah's thoughts. "You're just scared of death."

"I think I might have," Josiah heard his own voice get fainter. "Just a little."

"Well, you see what *little* that's worth." Bee tapped his cigar and ash dribbled onto Pollyanna's chin. "I'll keep an eye out for you on the TV, Preach. Something tells me that your next feature is going to be real entertaining."

Bee and Pollyanna were gone before Josiah even finished processing the words. They did not vanish; it was more like they had never been there to begin with.

The smoke pouring from the engine was even denser than before, and the gap underneath the crumpled hood spat out orange sparks that got lost in the atmosphere. It was time for him to go. In theory, he could drive until he found a payphone to call 911, but even as he got into his car, he knew that he was not going to try. Pollyanna would not be any less dead when the ambulance arrived. Her face would still be covered in blood.

If he waited around and got wrapped up in police and paramedic questions, he would never make it to the studio in time. Then her death would be for nothing.

Josiah's car engine purred as he started it up and sped off. He held onto the steering wheel with both hands, thinking about Pollyanna and trying to search for how he felt. Because she was dead. He had to feel something. He dug deep through his emotions, grabbing all the memories that had her mark on them. He turned them over in his mind's eye and looked for all the parts of her face he had memorized, from the way her nose crinkled and the way the corners of her eyes gathered when she smiled, to the very particular way her neck swooped down and met her shoulders in a clean, soft line that always begged to be bitten. Nothing seemed to stir.

If anything, Josiah felt very empty. So maybe Bee had been right, after all.

Josiah turned the radio back on.

CHAPTER THIRTEEN

UNFORGIVING SERVANT

It was dawn by the time Josiah stumbled out of his car. He parked right behind the Buick out of habit and staggered into his house through the garage, leaning heavily on his crutch as he walked. Every bone felt broken. Every joint felt like it had been stretched like taffy, twisted into a new shape, and then shoved back into place.

He was not in the mood for Theo and, *God*, he knew that he was going to have to deal with him.

Like an excitable labrador, his boyfriend dashed into view as soon as the garage door shut. He came skidding to a halt on the linoleum, his colorful socks providing just enough traction to keep him from careening into the kitchen table. If he had been stewing at all over Josiah's absence, that crankiness seemed to evaporate as soon as they locked eyes.

"You look like hell, Rev," Theo said. Josiah couldn't help but let out a short, breathy laugh and shook his head.

"Yeah?" He dashed his hand through his hair. "Well, I feel like hell, too."

"What happened after the broadcast?" Theo shuffled closer, reaching out to take Josiah's blazer. "Or...do I want to know?" The kicked-puppy style of uncertainty, conflated with the fine thread of indignation in his voice, was running Josiah's last frayed nerve through a mandolin.

"Did I space out?" Josiah asked. He didn't know how much had changed, how far back Bee had really gone when he pulled at the cosmos' loose threads.

"It was more than that," Theo said. "You were acting like you couldn't talk, and your eyes started seizing. It felt like you were on camera like that forever, but I guess it was only a few seconds. They cut to a pre-recorded broadcast for the rest of the hour."

"That was decent of them," Josiah snorted.

"So, what happened?" Theo pressed. "I called the hospital, and they said that you weren't there. I called five separate times during the night until the receptionist got short with me. She told me that—"

"—That God would handle it?" Josiah finished for him. Theo gave him an odd look, but he nodded.

Josiah loosened up his bolo tie and started unbuttoning his shirt with his one free hand. His bed was so welcoming, but he did not want to lay down while he was arguably still filthy. "You should have more faith, Theo. As you can see, God took care of me just fine."

"Oh, don't give me that crap," Theo said. He caught Josiah's tie before it fell to the floor and looped it over his hand before following his boyfriend into the bedroom. "Are you going to explain to me why you are on a crutch, then? Does Mack just hand those out to anyone who has a stroke on set?"

Josiah froze. His fingers twitched over the small white button in the middle of his chest and he rested his fingers against the side, twisting it thoughtfully rather than pushing it through its loop. Of course, he had to remind himself—Theo did not know. And he never went digging around in Josiah's closets.

"Theo," Josiah changed the subject. "Pollyanna is dead." He did not know how to make his voice sound anything other than deadpan. He was usually so good at putting on the showman personality, even in times of crisis. Not this time, for some reason. He could not do it.

Josiah stared at his partner's face, waiting for a reaction. He finished unbuttoning his shirt and tossed it onto the floor just to watch Theo bend to pick it up. His boyfriend stooped to the task without hesitation, maintaining a carefully blank expression the entire time.

Theo finally straightened his back and draped the dress shirt over his arm, looking Josiah in the eyes while he set down his crutch and pulled off his sweaty binder.

"I am sorry to hear that," Theo said. There was not a scrap of true chagrin to be found in his tone. "How did it happen?"

"She was driving home," Josiah told him. "She went off the road and hit a rail." It was partially true, at least.

He could tell by looking at Theo's face that his boyfriend did not believe him. Josiah sat down on the bed to kick off his trousers and Theo knelt in front of him, grabbing the fabric legs.

Theo looked up at him and pulled Josiah's pants down his thighs, sliding them along his calves until they were off completely. He added them to the little pile he had dropped into his lap without breaking eye contact.

"I am sorry," Theo said again. He looked like the yearlings that Josiah's uncle used to shoot. "I know how much she meant to you."

There it was, the underlying snark. Theo acted like Josiah could not taste it, like his words were not acid droplets burning holes into the preacher's skin.

Three years together and he had developed a hell of a lot of nerve.

The flash of anger felt good. It was something that Josiah could hold onto, better than feeling nothing at all. He thought about laying it all out for Theo. He thought about telling him exactly how much *better* Pollyanna had been at many things. He thought about mentioning her perfumed skin and her perfect ringlets, and about how comforting her presence was whenever he dreaded going home. It might have killed Theo to know that Josiah fantasized about going down on Pollyanna so carnally that he once caught himself starting to drool in the middle of an altar call.

Instead, what came out of Josiah's mouth was, "Do you know how much money I spent on her?"

Theo went still. "How much?" he asked. His words were so tight that the last syllable squeaked as it slid out.

"Well," Josiah began to count the gifts off on his fingers. "There was the Parisian perfume, the diamond necklace, the calfskin Bible that I had engraved..."

"Stop it!" Theo stood, clutching Josiah's dirty clothes against his chest. "Shut up, shut up! You're awful to me, Josiah Tucker!"

"At least I never gave her my credit card," Josiah said, adding malicious enunciation to each word.

Theo's nostrils flared. "Oh," he said. "Here it is. I don't have access to your bank account, Josiah. How was I supposed to pay for anything?"

"A monthly allowance wasn't enough?" Josiah snapped. "Well, apparently not. Because whatever you needed *so damn badly* did finally add up to twenty grand before they cut you off."

"I am not a child who should depend on an allowance!" Theo threw the bundle of dirty clothes. They hit Josiah in the face, and he sent them to the floor. "How many times have we had this same conversation? I am so *sick* of it...!" He wrapped his arms around his chest, a self-soothing habit he had developed that only made him look like he was pouting.

"Which conversation are we having, now?" Josiah asked. "Is it the one that ends with you crying? I suppose I shouldn't ask. It's not like that narrows things down."

"I cried for three days without eating or sleeping when the credit card company sent you that statement." Theo said. "I told you that I was sorry, in fact, I begged for your forgiveness. That is over, now, you promised me it was in the past!"

"Of course it is," Josiah said. "A lot of things are, now." He had his right hand balled into a fist, fighting back his own desire to scream in his boyfriend's face. "A few more things are about to be."

Theo stared at him. "What are you saying?" he asked.

"Not what you think," Josiah snapped out his heated trance long enough to give Theo a real answer. He looked his boyfriend up and down and then kicked the rumpled clothes on the floor. "I am going to take a shower," he said. "Believe it or not, I think I should try to sleep before I go back to the studio tonight."

"I think you should," Theo said. "You are being mean. I am willing to chalk that up to the fact that you're tired." He glanced down at the pile of clothes and then bent, again, to pick them up.

Josiah stood up. His hips protested by sending a sharp knife of pain down the front of his left leg.

Theo did not leave the room. Josiah just raised a tired brow at him and turned to walk into the attached bathroom.

At the sight of the shower, Josiah let out an exhausted sigh. He sat down on the edge of the tub and started the water, holding his hand under the spigot to monitor the temperature. It had to be a certain level of warmth before he would risk getting sprayed by the showerhead.

"Rev?" Theo was back to using the epithet, the one that replaced 'baby' and 'darling' and 'sweetheart' for anyone listening. "You don't ever want me to lie to you, right?"

"I would prefer it if you didn't," Josiah said, too bone-weary to feed into another argument. "Lying is a sin, etcetera."

"All right," Theo was quiet for half a second more, then Josiah heard him speak again over the water. "I am glad that your secretary is dead."

Josiah growled, but Theo did not seem to care if he noticed. The bedroom darkened as the thick brown curtains were drawn, and then Josiah heard the bedroom door slam shut.

He probably did not need to, but Josiah popped a sleep aid pill regardless. He did not want to risk dreaming about Pollyanna. He just wanted a few hours of solid, deep, dreamless sleep before he had to go make concessions to the devil.

Josiah slammed down a glass of water, set his alarm, and buried his face into his pillow. Either the pill was fast-acting, or his exhaustion was just too heavy to let him keep moving. He was not the most comfortable, and breathing was a little bit tricky through the pillowcase, but he simply could not move. His last thought before his eyelids came crashing down was '*I could always die in my sleep*.'

He did not die, but he did dream.

He was standing on a mountaintop overlooking a parched desert. The sky was the color of blood, interrupted only occasionally by narrow swatches of yellow in the form of drifting clouds that rippled over the carbon black sun like flames over a coal. Josiah could see every detail on the sun, for some reason, including every pit and crater that textured its surface. It was important to recognize that he could see it. The only reason that came to mind was '*God's Eye*.'

A spark of orange appeared in the center of the sun and started growing, like the lit end of a cigarette smoldering from a deep inhale. The spark became enormous, sweeping flames that trailed across the sky in ribbons, and in their center was a bright gold sphere. The sphere began to melt and distort, barreling through the sky and aiming for the very spot where he was standing. Josiah was not afraid, for some reason. He watched the sphere change form and felt nothing except an overwhelming sense of calm.

Josiah knew the flames were cool to the touch, but he was still unbearably hot. Sweat poured down his temples, soaking his hair and streaming over his upper lip. All he could taste was the bitterness of his own salt while the gold sphere continued to take its shape, picking up speed with every passing second.

The gold mass dove and swept over his head. Josiah threw himself to the ground to avoid being crushed by the massive twin wheels that had formed. As it went by, he glimpsed the underbelly of a chariot.

A flaming chariot, the likes of which God had sent down to take home the prophet Elijah. Every molecule in Josiah's body went numb with fear.

He trembled on all fours, lowering his head until his face was pressed against the dirt. He wished that he could will himself to sink deep into the earth and disappear. He wanted to pray that the chariot would keep going, that it would not turn around and return to the mountain, but he could not form the words.

146

Every sound that came out of his mouth was pure jibberish, with all the clarity of a church elder speaking in tongues.

The chariot came to rest on the ground next to him while the flames cast red light that made the surrounding rocks and bushes look bloody. Josiah was compelled to raise his head. The radiant, burning gold was blinding and he hissed in pain as it seared his eyes. They were hot and swollen when he closed them, and then he cupped one hand against his brow to shade them so he could try again.

Josiah cracked open his eyes only a fourth of the way the second time, his vision filtered through a curtain of lashes. The chariot came to a complete stop, and it was close enough that he could make out silver words emblazoned on the side. They were not letters he recognized, but he still understood their meaning to be *'False Prophet'.*

Josiah raised his head a little higher. There was someone standing at the front of the chariot draped all in white, with skeletal hands, so pale that they were almost blue, sticking out from the billowing sleeve. He tried searching for their face, but another bolt of fear struck him down. He let out a muffled cry and landed on his face in the dirt. His nose burned and throbbed from where it hit the ground.

Underneath the roaring flames, he heard a soft chattering. It was the sound of a hundred thousand voices trying to talk over each other at once. They were all varying pitches, some softer and some more resonant than others, and they all blended together into a dull, buzzing hum.

Without looking back up, Josiah reached out with one trembling hand. His fingers crept across the dirt before brushing up against something impossibly soft and cool. It was plush like velvet and slick like satin, and it ran like cool water underneath his fingertips.

The figure in the chariot let out a horrendous shriek. Josiah's head came up, pulled too far back like there was an invisible hand gripping him by the hair. Every bone in his neck cracked painfully, and Josiah was left staring up at the sky, straight into the carbon black sun.

The chariot launched itself back into the air and circled his head. It left golden rings around the black sun, and the brilliant light made his eyes burn and water. He tried to close them, but not a single muscle on his face twitched. He could not move anything. He was just staring up into the sky, helpless and paralyzed.

The figure in the chariot leaned over and glanced down at him. Underneath the flowing white fabric, Josiah caught the slightest glimpse of a face. Or, rather, what was barely a face. It looked more like a mask, smooth and white with only shadows where most features would be. The figure's skin looked like it was moving, like it was made of stretched linen and there was nothing but hands underneath it, writhing and pushing against the barrier while trying to claw free. Somewhere close to the chin, it looked like it had a mouth, but the whole structure was just a raw red gash with jagged, needle-like teeth and nothing to cover them.

The figure turned its head and pulled back the part of its hood that was covering the side of its face. Along the cheekbone and moving up the temple were three pale blue eyes, like a faded pattern on some dusty China, flickering around in different directions. The eye in the center stopped first and turned downward, and then the other two followed until all three irises were staring down at him.

The overlapped voices grew louder. Josiah still could not make sense of them. They climbed to such an impossible, piercing decibel that his ears rang and warmth started to leak out of their tunnels.

"False prophet, false Christ." The words sounded like they were coming from three different voices, all speaking at once. A sharp pain dug into the back of his hand and then dragged across the surface. More sticky, runny warmth. It flowed between his fingers and the pain came again. *"Beware of false prophets."*

Even though the figure was still in its chariot, staring down at him with three unblinking eyes, there was someone at his side. Josiah felt like someone was holding his hand, caressing it, and carving something into his skin at the same time.

The pain was enough to tear a cry out of his throat. He was amazed that he could open his mouth, considering how only moments before he had not been able to move his lips. "I am no deceiver!" Josiah gasped. Every desperate word jumbled the small bones in his throat that had been knocked loose. "I teach the Bible, all the words from God's mouth…!"

His words still did not make sense to his own ears. He knew what he was saying, but it came out in some other language, or just nonsense again like before. The pain in his hand increased. Whatever was cutting into him drove itself deeper and made his arm jerk involuntarily.

"Liar. Heretic. False teacher." The unified voices grew louder, grumbling like thunder. There was a new pain, like a blade was being driven through the center of his hand. Josiah screamed.

He opened his eyes, for real this time, but he could not move. There was a sliver of light coming from the side of the thick curtain and the beam hit him right in the face. His forehead was drenched in sweat and so were the sheets clinging to his bare legs. Josiah drew in a deep breath through his nose in an effort to force himself to stay calm. He tried to call out, but his jaw was locked, and the only sound he could make was a loud groan. He kept trying to roll onto his side and drag his arm up with him. It was unbearably hot in the sunlight, which only made him more miserable.

It felt like an hour before his body gave up and released him. Josiah managed to swing his arm over and the motion flipped him onto his back. He did not realize he had wiggled over so close to the edge of the bed until the moment he rolled off the side and almost landed on his face. Josiah managed to catch himself with his hand and, even though the impact hurt like hell, it was better than hitting his nose.

As he moved to sit up, Josiah's alarm went off above his head. He muttered a string of obscenities under his breath as he slammed his aching hand down against the snooze button.

His head hurt and the room felt like it was spinning. All he really wanted was to go back to bed, but that was not an option. He had to get ready.

God only knew what would happen to him if he was late.

CHAPTER FOURTEEN

THE LOWEST SEAT

There were three types of preachers, as far as Josiah had identified. You had your down-to-earth preachers, those small-town boys whose only mission statement was to serve their reclusive communities and spread the gospel far and wide. They drove almost-new pickup trucks and rotated out the same three suits that their wives continued to mend until they passed around the offering plate for a new one. They fit into the category that Josiah liked to call *'Trailer Park Pastors'.* Their sermons were like homecooked meals, familiar, filling, and rarely flavorful.

Then, you had your middle-tier preachers. They were the *'Suburban'* type. They drove SUV's and their churches sent out monogrammed vans to low-income neighborhoods for Sunday morning transportation. They had a few more suits, always one that they insisted was designer because it had come from the most expensive department store. Their sermons were more like fast food, comforting and insubstantial. Always left you wanting just enough to bring you back.

Then, you had your preachers of Josiah's category: *'Hollywood'.* Portraying the role of a Holy celebrity was part of the package, and it came with a lot of suits. His walk-in closet was filled with them, some that were still hanging in the bags they had arrived in. A lot of them cost more than most first-tier pastors caught in their collection plates. In fact, a visiting pastor with leather patches on the elbows of his badly-cut blazer once took a hard look at

Josiah's suit and said starkly, "my church could pay its light bill with that".

The only response Josiah gave him was, "Twice."

Hollywood Preacher sermons were the candy bars of the industry. Always something new, always something exciting, always something you could not stop swallowing.

Josiah pulled out a white suit with thin black pinstripes running down the blazer and matching trousers. He chose a red collared shirt to go with it and a gold bolo tie, laying it all out on the bed before dressing. He would wear his white cowboy boots, the ones that made all the blue-collar workers in the congregation roll their eyes.

He put a dangling diamond-encrusted cross in one ear and a diamond stud through the other. He put on a new gold-plated watch with more diamonds around the face, and he slipped on every ring in his immediate line of sight. He spritzed cologne on every pulse point, as if a touch of *'Black Suede'* would be enough to cover up the smell of his fear.

He took his time. To a certain extent, it was all about more than just the presentation. He wanted to linger as long as possible in his home—the dream house that he had bought outright only three years prior, and around the same time he started dating Theo. Everything had gone downhill so quickly. He wondered how quickly he would lose it all after the devil's desired broadcast aired.

Pollyanna was dead. Theo would probably leave. Still, things had a lot of room to get worse.

Josiah dipped his fingers in oil and used it to encourage curls at the ends of his hair. He shaved his face. He brushed his teeth.

As he spat into the sink, he thought, *'I really need to go.'*

He took one last look at himself in the mirror, buttoning his blazer so that it hugged his middle and made his shoulders look even broader.

When Josiah turned to leave the room, Theo was standing in the doorway. He had both hands out, pressed against the frame to block his boyfriend in. Josiah picked up his Bible and faced his partner.

"Theo," he said, "I have to get to the studio."

"No," Theo said, bringing down one hand to adjust his glasses. "I have decided that you are not going tonight. You are going to stay home, and we are going to talk things out."

"There is nothing left to talk about," Josiah tried not to sound irate, but his patience had already burnt down its fuse. "And it is not as simple as 'don't go'. This is my job, Theo!"

"I. Do. Not. *Care.*" Theo snarled the last word, sounding like he was on the verge of tears. "You have never once chosen me, Josiah. I have never been the most important thing in your life. But now I am here telling you what I need, and I want you to prioritize me just this *once!*"

Josiah held onto his Bible like it was the only thing keeping him together. "Honey," he said while barely able to unclench his teeth, "I need to do this. I will come home, and we will talk about it."

"You always say that." Theo shot back. "You never, ever follow through. So why should I believe you this time?"

"What is it going to take?" Josiah made sure there was only a hair's breadth of distance between them. He recognized the look in Theo's eyes. It was a look that he had captured in his own during the many times he was left sitting on the bathroom sink after a fight with Brooks, holding a bag of ice against his bruised arm. "You have won, Theo. Pollyanna is gone, and I've got no one else, so you don't have any reason to get so worked up."

"For one thing," Theo said, "I don't believe that you have 'no one else'. We both acted like I did not know about her, but I did, and you were willing to keep lying to me. How do I know that she was the only other person you've been fucking? And also—"

"No," Josiah cut him off. "There is no 'and also', Theo. I need to leave. I need to work. I will come back after the broadcast."

"And how can I know that?" Theo challenged, sticking out his chin.

Josiah thought about wielding the Bible like a club and knocking his boyfriend in the head with it.

"Do you remember when we started dating?" Josiah asked. That seemed to throw his boyfriend for a loop. Theo blinked, a little too slowly, before he answered.

"We met in a club," Theo said. "I stole my friend's shot when he went to the bathroom, and you said..."

"That I could keep your secret," Josiah finished, "if you could keep mine."

"You've always said that night made you feel like you were on top of the world," Theo said.

"It did," Josiah said. "There was nothing but 8-balls and vodka in my system that night. That isn't the point. You trusted me, then, and you didn't know me."

"I trust you less now that I do," Theo sighed. "You used to trust me, too."

"It seems we are both bad judges of character," Josiah said. "For example, you seem to think that I will not take the word of the Lord and deliver it straight to your head the old-fashioned way."

"I don't think any such thing," Theo said. "But I know that if you hit me, Josiah, I am going to walk right out that door. Maybe I will, anyway. Maybe I won't be here when you come back from work."

"That's fine," Josiah said. He plowed forward and bumped his shoulder into Theo's, forcing his boyfriend back and into the hallway. Theo offered no resistance. He staggered when Josiah pushed him and stared after his partner in disbelief.

"You really don't care." Theo sounded equal measures of hurt and unbelievably furious.

"I don't." Josiah barely looked at him again before walking away. He echoed Bee's sentiment. "There will always be another twink."

The studio parking lot was empty, and it should not have been. The inside was dark, from what Josiah could tell, and all the doors were closed. He found his parking spot, anyway, and took his time walking up to the door. He left his crutch inside the Corvette, even though his hips sent up pangs of regret only seconds after. He kept his movements at a leisurely stroll, like it was just another Sunday and here he was, just a man of God enjoying a glorious evening.

When Josiah reached the nearest doors, he reached out to grab the handle to see if they were locked. He barely touched it before the door swung open, inviting him into the cool, dark depths.

Josiah fidgeted with his bolo tie and stepped inside. The cold air was very welcome as it greeted his hot skin, but it did nothing to ease the fear that had settled in the pit of his stomach and formed a ball of ice. He felt it rolling around while he walked, squeezing the lining of his guts until he was clenching every muscle to keep from letting his bowels run the show.

He knew his way around the studio pretty well, but in the darkness, everything looked the same. Josiah held one hand out as he walked, trying to keep himself from crashing into anything as he searched for any sign of the devil's whereabouts. The watch on his wrist stopped ticking, and its sudden silence was like a hammer being dropped.

Without the steady hands of his watch, Josiah could not tell whether it was for minutes or hours that he walked in circles around the pitch-black studio. Finally, he gave up on looking and found a stool to sit on while he waited. His eyes adjusted enough that when he held his watch close to his face, he could make out the golden numerals set in white. He tried twisting the knob on his watch around like that would fix the problem, but all it did was turn the hands every which way until they landed back in their original position.

He was so transfixed that a sudden burst of static knocked him off his seat.

Josiah hit the floor. He landed on his back, this time, and something cracked in an unforgiving way. He hissed in pain and rolled over onto his side, gingerly pushing himself up.

A TV sat in front of him, almost as big as his own, and it was bleeding ghoulish blue light. The static on the screen was unbearably loud, the sound itself like claws digging into the back of his skull. Josiah gnashed his teeth and crawled towards the TV, reaching out for the nearest dial that would hopefully turn it off.

Before he could touch it, the static cleared away. A picture appeared with his nose only inches away from the screen. Josiah found himself staring at the phosphors that formed a face exactly like his, one that was nodding and smiling with features that became too blurry to discern whenever it looked the camera head-on.

When it spoke to him, it was nothing but fuzzy black holes for eyes and a gaping, dark mouth that an odd white line kept knocking out of alignment.

"I HAVE TO ADMIT IT, SWEETHEART, I DIDN'T THINK YOU WOULD COME." The voice on the television screen sounded just like his, yet the mouth barely moved.

"I almost doubted it, myself," Josiah breathed. He moved his face up and felt the static from the screen tickle his nose.

"DEALER'S CHOICE, THEN. WHAT IS IT GOING TO BE?" The TV changed, flashing a picture of a rooster and then a picture of a cat.

Josiah made a face. "What does that mean?" He pulled himself onto his knees and sat back, looking around. "Are you going to fuck me from all the way over there?"

The TV switched off. The room was pitch black again, but only for a moment. All the studio lights came on at once, and Josiah winced.

The TV was gone, and in its place was a microphone. It was plated in gold, not a studio mic by any means, and had his name engraved on the side. In curling script it read, *'Reverend Josiah Tucker'.*

"Pick it up," the voice no longer sounded like his. It was much closer to the voice that had greeted him at the crossroads six years ago. It sounded like it was coming from every direction at once, like it was both far away and also right up against his ear.

Josiah did as he was told. The mic was heavier than he expected, and he held it in both hands.

"What am I supposed to do with this?" He asked.

"Take it over to the set," the devil said. "I want you to fuck yourself with it."

Heat flooded Josiah's face, but he blamed the studio lights as he walked over to the set. It was dressed with a baroque-style armchair, dark cherry wood and plush green padding. It was the chair that Mack liked for him to sit in when delivering sad news, like a soldier death count or a cancer diagnosis.

Josiah looked around one more time before pulling down his pants. He sat down in the armchair and held the mic in front of him, looking at the base with some doubt.

"Don't think you can fit it?" The voice came directly across from him. Josiah looked up and saw himself standing there by a large camera, grinning like a cheshire cat and wearing the exact same suit that Josiah had chosen.

The only difference was in the bolo ties. Josiah's was shaped like a cross, the devil's was shaped like a bat.

"It will fit," Josiah said. "But there is no lube."

The devil's grin widened.

"All right," the devil said. "Then give it some."

It took a moment for Josiah to realize what he meant, but then he lowered his head and started to wrap his mouth around the mic's base.

"No, no." The devil stopped him. "Hold up your head and face the camera. Do it nice and slow. Also, use the other side."

"The other side?" Josiah wasn't sure he heard right.

"Yes." A long, pointed red tail slithered out from underneath the devil's coat and wrapped around the camera, adjusting the lens. "I turned the sound on for a reason."

Josiah took a deep breath. "Is this live?" he asked.

"Suck the damn microphone." The devil clicked his tongue.

Josiah turned the mic around and pressed the head against his lips. He dragged his tongue over the mesh and the sound echoed around him ten times louder than he was used to.

"That's a bit better," the devil said. Josiah tried not to roll his eyes as he kept going. He swiped his tongue all the way around and dragged it up behind his teeth until he had his whole mouth wrapped around it. Josiah sucked on the mic, and every awful squelching sound that came out of it made his ears itch. When Josiah pulled it free, the mesh was glistening, and his tormenter was adjusting the lens again.

"All right," the devil said. "Now, go for it."

Josiah tried to keep his focus on breathing steadily as he spread his legs apart. He pressed the mic up against his first hole, knowing that would be an easier task, but he could not bring himself to push it in. He slid it down to the second and leaned back a little farther, spreading his legs and pulling them up until they were flung across the arms of the chair. He pressed the mic against his tight hole and his breaths started coming up shorter. It was not going to fit.

"It won't fit," he said. "I know that it won't."

The devil did not say anything in response. He simply waited, patiently, while the spit on the mic was drying up faster than Josiah's hesitation.

There was no way out. He just had to do it. Josiah closed his eyes and tried to relax as much as possible, pressing the head up the mic once more against his entrance. He tried to work it in, but his sphincter was unyielding, and he finally had to grit his teeth and shove it inside.

The pain made it feel like he had ripped himself a new hole. Josiah grunted in pain and tried to hold back his discomfort as he pushed the mic in as far as it could go. Once he could not get it in any further, he held it there for just a second before pulling it back. It did not feel any better coming out, and he stopped just before he could yank the head free entirely. He shoved it back inside, then back out, then back in. His thighs shook as he fucked himself with the microphone, and he had to listen to every minute of it.

"That's not too bad." The devil's voice was like hot wax dripping over his genitals. "Although I think it would be better if you came."

Josiah accepted the covert instruction and put his other hand into play. He found his cock and started rubbing it, making hard, fast circles to try and get himself there as quickly as possible. If this was all the devil wanted, it could be bearable, he might find a way back from this. The thoughts of where his humiliation could be playing, how many living rooms could be watching, were so distracting that every potential orgasm kept slipping away. He chased it until his cock was chaffed and his other hand was cramping from fucking his ass with the microphone. When he could not take it anymore, he swapped hands, shoving two fingers in his mouth and swirling his tongue around them to try and get more lubrication.

At last, he came. It was a pitiful orgasm, but he was finally overstimulated enough that when he let up on the pressure, a few soft strokes were enough to make him shoot off. Josiah cried out in relief and pulled the mic out, going faster than he should have in his hurry. He felt something else tear.

"God!" Josiah dropped the mic onto the floor and pulled his knees in. His whole body was shaking as he rubbed his face.

"That bad, hm?" the devil asked. He had such cold, empty blue eyes. Josiah wondered if his were that empty.

"I did it," Josiah said on a ragged breath. "I did what you wanted; I paid your due."

"Not even close, sweetheart, but that was a nice try," the devil said. "You might as well take the rest of your clothes off, because you have a lot of making up to do."

CHAPTER FIFTEEN

COST OF DISCIPLESHIP

Panic and disgust clawed at his chest. He had to leave. He had to pull up his pants and walk away. Josiah tried to stand, but his legs buckled immediately. He fell to his knees and felt a hand grab him by the hair, gripping him close to the scalp. The smell of tobacco and something like cloves assaulted his nose and made him choke. Another hand wrapped around his throat, pressing into the soft parts just behind the corners of his jaw and squeezing.

"You're being such a princess about this," the devil scoffed. He lowered Josiah to the ground until the reverend was flat on his back. "You have a lot of nerve for someone who is bleeding out of his ass."

"Is this your ideal scene?" Josiah spat. "Is this everything you thought it would be?"

The devil tilted his head. "No," he said. "I thought I would be having more fun. But you're very wet, and not in a good way."

Josiah had not expected to take such a blow to his ego, but he found himself suddenly indignant over the implication that he was a bad lay. "I would say that you are the one with a lot of nerve," he pointed out. "Talking like that when you haven't even touched me for yourself."

"You're right," the devil purred. Josiah could not look past the face that was so sickeningly identical to his own. He saw his own head tilt down until his eyes were peering up from underneath dark brows, and he saw his own limbs stretch out to straddle his hips, every movement as graceful as a cat.

The devil rolled his shoulders and stripped off the white pinstripe blazer. He tossed it aside like it was nothing and then slid his bolo tie down, maintaining eye contact with every movement.

Josiah's panic fluttered again in his chest. "Why not use your own face?" he asked. Anything to distract himself from what was about to happen.

The devil laughed. "Because I want you to get off," he said. "And you can only do that when you are looking at yourself."

"That is not true," Josiah said.

The devil ripped his shirt open down the middle, popping every button and sending them scattering into every corner. Unlike Josiah, he was not wearing a binder. His hairy chest, the round B-cup that it was, was on full display with gold straight barbells pierced through his dusky pink nipples.

"I know you," the devil said, "better than you know yourself." He rolled his hips, grinding down on Josiah's crotch before lifting himself up to remove his trousers.

A deep, needy twinge struck the walls of Josiah's entrance and made his whole system clench. The aftermath of the twinge felt like guilt.

"Do you?" Josiah hated how breathy his voice sounded. He cleared his throat to try and strengthen it. "I need something to call you. Someone asked for your name, once, and I had nothing to give outside of a Biblical answer."

"Yes, I know. What was it you gave Bee, again? Holden?" Completely naked, the devil stretched himself out over Josiah's body. His skin was so hot that Josiah could have sworn it was letting off steam. "I like that. That is fine."

Holden, the devil, lowered his hips so that they were grinding against Josiah's once again. He reached down and spread himself apart just enough that his clit could rub against Josiah's red, overstimulated one. The devil's clit was bigger and thicker, and about an inch longer, so that when he slid a little bit farther down he was dangerously close to slipping inside of the preacher.

Josiah moaned and grabbed hold of the devil's hips, digging his fingers into his round, tight ass. Holden was soaking wet, and his clit's journey up and down Josiah's sensitive cock was a slippery one. Josiah writhed underneath him, wanting more and hating himself for that. Holden straightened and hovered over Josiah's hips, holding himself

172

there for just a moment before lowering himself back down and grinding against him. Now it was Josiah who was so tantalizingly close to sliding inside of the man on top of him. His cock ached, and he wanted a dozen things at once. He wanted to be fucked, he wanted to be sucked off—but above all, he wanted to cum. Again, and again, and again.

"Greed..." The devil's hot breath traveled over his ear and the words caressed him with the touch of a lover. "You are a greedy boy, Josiah Tucker."

"Stop it," Josiah growled through his teeth. "I want you to fuck me."

"I know." The devil leaned over and caught Josiah's face in his hands. "And you're so used to getting what you want."

Holden's mouth was as scalding as a brand. His kiss had the same bite as hot metal, and his tongue filled the inside of Josiah's mouth like boiling oil. Josiah screamed at the contact, but the devil's tongue muffled most of his protest. When Holdren drew back, Josiah's mouth was still hanging open, his lips painfully blistered and oozing blood down his chin.

"Holy fuck!" Josiah held his hand over his mouth, but the heat from his palm only made the burning worse. "Fuck, shit-!"

"Do you have a swear jar at your house?" the devil asked idly. "I think you need one." He slid down the length of Josiah's body and pushed his legs apart, teasing the inside of his thigh with a stream of hot breath. Every muscle in Josiah's body seized with panic at the idea of what happened to his mouth happening to his cock, and he closed his thighs around Holden's head.

The devil laughed. "I wasn't going to," he said. He dipped his fingers between Josiah's legs and started stroking his cock, using the leftover wetness from his own slick thighs to work his fingers up into fast, tight circles. "Can you see the camera?"

Josiah barely registered the question. He arched his back and pushed himself down onto the devil's fingers, craning his neck to catch a glimpse of the dark camera lens above his head. "Yes," he moaned.

"Good." Holden's voice was back to being a smooth, velvety purr. "I want you to look right into it. Just like that." His fingers picked up speed, and he used his other to tease Josiah's second hole. Josiah was still sore, and when

Holden pushed his fingers inside, it was like being ripped open all over again. He groaned again in pain but spread his legs, careful to keep his eyes on the camera lens. He could sort of see his face, but most of his vision was consumed by the dark, wide lens.

It made it easier to focus on the orgasm that was building quickly between his legs. It was as if Holden had his fingers tangled in every nerve strung throughout Josiah's body and he was pulling them all down to the tip of his cock. Each stroke of the devil's fingers sent such a violent wave of pleasure through Josiah that he gave into convulsions. His body was completely out of his control. His legs and arms shook, his hips jerked and his back arched. He choked on a sermon's worth of unsaid pleas until he could no longer swallow and spit was pouring out the side of his mouth. The devil's fingers alternated between stroking him and thrusting inside of him, moving in rapid succession so that he was unable to linger on one sensation for too long. Josiah's head was past the point of spinning. It felt completely detached. He was barely able to keep his eyes focused on the camera, with how hard they were trying to roll up inside of his head.

"That's much better," Holden cooed. "You know, you're prettier when you don't talk. If you lose it all, maybe you can start over as porn star."

Josiah cried out in frustration, but even his agitation was no match for the pleasure that had a vice-like grip on every bodily function.

The orgasm finally started to crest. Josiah was getting closer and closer, and he clenched around the devil's fingers, intent on riding it out to the end.

Holden started to pull his fingers back, and Josiah screamed.

"No!" Josiah's arms flailed and he clawed at the floor. "Give it to me!"

"Say please." The devil's voice was passionless as he stared down at Josiah with those flat, cold eyes.

"What?" Josiah asked desperately.

"Say please," the devil repeated.

"Oh, my God. Please, please!" Josiah ground down onto the devil's hand again. Holden finally smiled and thrust his hand against the reverend, fucking him with his fingers. Josiah's words were reduced to stammering.

"Please, please, fuck! Yes! Please, oh, let me, let me, please-!"

"Tell the truth about who you are," the devil said. "You're a sinner and a sodomite."

"I-mm!"

"What was that, reverend?"

"God, yes, I'm a sinner!" Josiah moaned, close to tears.

"They're just numbers to you, aren't they? You don't give a shit about anyone on the other side of that TV screen. They're just here to fund your greasy habits. Tell them that."

"I don't, I don't!" Josiah was past lightheaded. He barely felt real. "I don't give a shit about them!"

"Mhm, there we are. That wasn't so hard, was it? The truth will set you free, oh yes, you can come for me," the devil said.

Josiah could not hold it back. As soon as permission was given, he cried out and gushed all over himself. The devil continued to stroke him and fuck him, not letting up even as the orgasm built up again. It was more painful the second time around, but pleasure had enough of an edge that Josiah was able to release again, and again.

"That's right. Oh, that's good. You're so good when you wait for permission. Look at you, sweetheart." The devil's voice was as good as a warm, wet tongue between his legs.

He lost track of how many times he came before Holden finally pulled his hands back and Josiah was left laying on the floor, staring up into the camera and feeling like he had been yanked inside out.

"I bet that was one for the nightly news," Holden said. His voice was farther away, now. Josiah had lost track of everything. He had gone from looking into the camera to staring at the ceiling and trying not to think too hard. He was not brave enough to feel between his legs and assess the damage.

"I don't think that's the sort of thing they can show on public television," Josiah finally managed to respond. His whole body hurt so badly. He was not sure how he was going to stand up. "What happens now?"

"That's up to you," the devil said. "I—well. That is disappointing."

"What?" Josiah asked. He sat up too quickly and his world dipped.

"It doesn't look like we were on air after all," the devil said. He held up a length of film to demonstrate his point. "It looks like I recorded everything instead."

Josiah's breath caught in his throat. "So, what does that mean?" He asked.

The devil shrugged. "I'm a perfectionist," he said. "So, it looks as though we will have to do it all again."

CHAPTER SIXTEEN

KINGDOM OF HEAVEN

"**W**ait." Josiah held up his hand. The thought of having another orgasm made him nauseous. He was not sure that he could physically bear it. He was so tender and swollen between his thighs. "That can't be right. I paid what was due. It should be done, regardless. I held up my end."

"Perhaps." The devil's tail flicked into view out of nowhere and curled around his thigh as he spoke. "But neither you nor I are accustomed to stopping before we get what we want, *exactly* how we want it." He ripped the film out of the camera and let it fall to the floor.

"You like to compare us," Josiah said, mustering enough lingering hatred to give the devil a dark look. "We are nothing alike."

"We have our differences," Holden admitted. "For one, you never feel like you have enough time. I know differently. Time is just a game, like everything else."

"You would say that." Josiah reached behind him to grab his pants. "You are divine, and therefore immortal. Time isn't anything to you."

Holden blinked at him, as if Josiah had just regurgitated his own words. "Yes," the devil said. "I am divine, and you are impatient." He finished fiddling with the camera and then walked over to another. "If you are worried that I am going to come for you again right this moment, don't be. Take a moment to rest. And we can get more creative next time. You're not as drippy as I thought."

"I don't know how to take that," Josiah said.

"You take most things pretty well," the devil told him. "I never thought I would say this, but you should have more confidence in yourself."

Still seated on the floor, Josiah put his back to the chair and leaned against it. He closed his eyes and tried to take a deep breath, but his chest hurt so much that it stopped short, and he felt dizzy all over again.

"How long are we going to be here?" he asked, already drifting off.

"Impatient." Holden's voice sounded even farther away than before. "Just like I said."

It did not feel good to see the studio parking lot empty. Josiah pulled into his space and turned off his car, looking around to see if he could catch a glimpse of anything at all, even if it was Mack's avocado-green topless menace. There was nothing.

Even the inside of the studio looked dark. Josiah took his time getting out of the car and walking up to the door. He left his crutch in the seat beside him out of pride, but it did not take him long to regret his decision.

When he finally reached the door, Josiah grabbed the handle to see if it was locked. The door opened easily, hissing quietly on oiled hinges, and he was greeted by a gust of cold air.

Something hit him in the stomach, fear or dread or maybe both. Whatever the feeling was, it was chilling enough to make him let go of the door.

The door did not swing closed, although it stayed open only as much as he had pulled it back. Josiah hesitated but grabbed the handle again and waited for the feeling to return. The sense of dread had vanished. The flash of fear simmered down to more usual nerves.

Josiah shook his head and let himself in.

As it appeared from the outside, none of the lights were on. Josiah kept one hand out in front of him as he waited for his eyes to adjust, walking slowly and trying not to run into anything.

"Where are you?" he muttered, stretching his arm out further into the darkness.

'Right here.' The answer came in the form of a cold breeze skittering up his spine. A foreign set of fingers appeared in the darkness and threaded their way between his own, gripping his whole hand.

Josiah felt like he had swallowed his whole heart. He jerked his arm back, but the other hand held tightly onto his.

"Come on, reverend." The voice sounded like his own, and it coaxed him into the darkness with the same honeyed wheedling he used to get congregates to whip out their checkbooks. "You don't need to be afraid. This is nothing you haven't done before."

That feeling hit him again, coupled with a damning sense of déjà vu. Josiah's next succession of breaths came a little faster.

"I've been here before," he said.

"Yes, sweetheart. You work here," the devil reminded him.

"No." Josiah tried to focus on that trail of thought, but his senses were slipping away faster than he could speak. "That's not it."

A pair of eyes appeared, the same shape as his, except the irises were gold. "This is important, Reverend." The voice continued to lure him in, along with the insistent tug from the devil's hand. "This is for your whole career.

Whatever it takes, right? That's how it has always been."

"Whatever it takes." Josiah's sigh ended in a groan, and he rolled his head around on his neck. "All right, all right. Let's get it over with."

The devil's hand slid away and was replaced by cold metal. The studio lights came on at the same time, a bright flash that nearly blinded him. Josiah winced and tried to focus on what had been left behind. The devil had handed him a mic, plated in gold. Nothing like one he had ever seen before.

The mesh on the head was crusted in blood.

"All right," the devil said, his voice sounding even more like Josiah's, if that was possible. He clapped his hands and raised them towards the ceiling, shaking them in a mockery of Josiah's more enthusiastic sermons. "Woo! Here we *go!* I have faith in this take, let me tell you. Not to be funny, but it must be a cold day in Hell for me to have faith in something."

"There is blood on this microphone," Josiah said, holding it up for inspection.

The devil did not even spare him a glance. "I want a real sermon from you, this time. So don't shove that up your ass, you lunatic. I want you to look into this camera and give me something from the heart. But I want you third knuckle deep in your own holes while you do it, have you got that?"

His sweaty hand left smears over the gold plating. Josiah's legs already felt like Jell-O.

"What if I can't?" Josiah asked. The devil paused.

"What *if* you can't?" he echoed back.

Josiah held the microphone tighter. "I can barely stand."

"Well, take your time," the devil said. "I'm in no rush. Some might argue that we have all the time in the cosmos."

A new emotion pulled at Josiah's chest; a deep, harrowing sadness. It clawed its way up his throat and threatened to bring out tears, but he refused to let them loose.

"How many times have I done this already?" he asked.

The devil only looked at him with those infernal golden eyes. His red tail swished behind him like a cat, curling and uncurling like a wisp of smoke in the air.

"I don't deserve this," Josiah said. His senses were already slipping away.

The devil still did not say anything. A bitter silence yawned between them and could have stretched on forever, but Josiah finally gave in. He moved to sit in the plush green chair, where the seat was hard and crusted in spots from fluids turned into streaks of white and dark red swathes of blood.

Josiah took off his pants and leaned against the back of the chair, pulling his legs up so that his feet rested against the edge of the cushion while he kept his thighs spread wide. Josiah pressed his fingers up against his second hole and was immediately zapped by burning agony.

The camera's dark, unforgiving lens stared him down. *'God's Eye',* he thought, although he was not sure why.

Already trembling from pain, Josiah put the mic up to his lips.

"My God is the God of Abraham, Isaac, and Jacob," he said. "All my sins have been washed away by the blood of His son and I fear *no* evil. Can I get an *a-men?*"

"A-men." The devil grinned and flicked his tongue.

ABOUT THE AUTHOR

SIRIUS (they/them) is the author of The Dread South Series, the Gentleman Demon series, the Wirekillers series, the Draonir Saga, and multiple short stories included in various anthologies and literary magazines. When not writing, they are spreading blasphemy as a drag king or doting on their beloved dogs.

www.ingramcontent.com/pod-product-compliance
Lightning Source LLC
Chambersburg PA
CBHW010545100726
47903CB00011B/3155